I0625776

A Masquerade Affair
By
Elin Magdalene

Dedicated with cherished memories to
My loving Mama and Papa:
You live on in us

Richard slid his arm over the backrest of the bench and turned slightly towards her, legs crossed. He was close enough that his breath fanned her cheek, warming and caressing it.

"I'm not sure that you made a wise choice coming out here alone."

"Why not?"

"Well, for one thing there could be sharks lurking somewhere on the beach," he joked.

"Do you mean the sharks that inhabit the ocean or the ones that roam the land?"

"I wasn't aware there were sharks roaming the land."

"Perhaps that's because it's *your* school."

He laughed. Sitting close to him, she felt butterflies flapping around with excitement in her stomach.

"And what do the sharks that roam the land prey on?" he asked huskily.

"You tell *me*. It's your school of fish."

"Pursue steamy, hot ladies with impressively beautiful legs, perhaps?"

Chapter One

Vivi swiveled her chair around when she heard a knock on the door. She had been looking out the window, pondering on possible changes that could impact her workplace.

The company she worked for, Weisener Enterprise was undergoing a merger. The leadership team had an upcoming conference with the new CEO, Richard Mcgallan. She was part of that team so she thought it would not hurt to search him up on the internet.

Her findings came as no surprise. The paparazzi could not resist covering his every activity. Character-wise, in her opinion, he did not possess the qualities of a CEO for a company like theirs, but she had to admit he *was* ridiculously photogenic or heart-crushingly handsome.

Howard Weisener, the soon to be former CEO, was hardly at the office lately although technically he had not retired yet. Before announcing his retirement, he had proposed a merger with a rival company. The board had voted in favor of the proposal and now the merger was in progress.

She was skeptical of men, matching the description of the incoming CEO, who she considered the rich, powerful, and egoistic. She knew, from personal experience, what happened when one fell on the receiving end of the actions of such men. The experience had left her scarred and it was one she would not want anyone to suffer.

She was brought out of her musings when Willie, her workmate, poked his head through the door.

He asked, "Did you get the email?"

"Which one?"

"The one with the change of plans on the meeting."

"Is it being postponed?"

"No, but the CEO is unable to attend the meeting so we will be meeting with the CFO."

Willie left her, closing the door quietly behind him as she pulled the chair over to her desk and browsed her emails. It was a recent one, sent about fifteen minutes earlier.

The email was brief and offered no apologies. It noted that in lieu of previous plans the CFO of Mcgallan Corporation would be meeting with them because the CEO had a pressing issue which had suddenly come up.

What a flimsy excuse for evading a critical meeting, she thought. Surely, he was aware of all that goes into a merger and how the lives of others are impacted? So...which part of it all was not considered "pressing issue" to be prioritized?

The main reason she had gone into corporate law in the first place was to protect others from ruthless, wealthy, men like him. She saw herself as an undercover agent for the employees. She gave legal advice that was in the best interest of both the company and the employees. So how would this merger impact her job?

Vivi sighed as she remembered the most challenging year of her life which influenced her career choice. She cringed at the thoughts clouding her mind as she recalled the price she'd had to pay to get her life back on track. Her hand reached up to rest tenderly on the heart-shaped locket cradled on her chest.

She was the daughter of a pastor and was held up to high standards. She was in the top one percent in her class, helped to care for the little kids during church, and had not so much as smiled with a boy as a teenager.

When she was sixteen, she had begun working at the church. She had saved her money for the trip she planned to make when she turned eighteen. She did everything right, in her parents' honor, until she became a legal adult.

At age eighteen, she had embarked upon a journey of discovery with her parents' consent. She had thought she could uphold her family's values wherever she went. Why did she not remain true to those values when it really mattered?

Instead, she had decided to discover her wild side for a short while. Just a little bit of fun but it was much more than she had bargained for. The consequences of that decision could not be securely tucked away.

Her eyes clouded with tears at the tough choices she had had to make since she made that trip. Were those tears of remorse or loss? If only tears could wash away the past. She brushed the tears away gently and reminded herself that the vulnerable eighteen-year-old had being transformed into a confident, extraordinarily successful lawyer. She would not hesitate to stand up for her rights and that of her fellow workmates even if the price she had to pay this time was her job.

Richard made his way through the bustling crowd at Los Angeles International Airport. He was glad to be back to seal the merger which his company had begun before his departure.

He hurried by, hoping to avoid journalists or fellow travelers excited to buy-in on celebrity gossips. It was obvious he was the focus of the conversations buzzing around him.

He heard cameras clicks but he ignored the endeavors to get close-up snaps of him and trusted his team of security to keep his private space cleared of intruders. He had gotten accustomed to such encounters because it came with his status.

Occasionally, he even smiled or waved to the paparazzi because he considered them allies in his line of business. He felt their publicity was an asset because they inadvertently advertised his business to the public.

As he made his way through a group of unwavering passersby, a voice called out, "Welcome back Mr. Mcgallan. Where are you from precisely?"

He could tell she was a journalist and he gave her credit for the audacity to get her question out.

Richard revealed one of his heart-melting smiles and responded, "Thank you. Just got back from Africa—Liberia to be precise."

He heard the follow up question, "And the purpose of your visit to Liberia, sir?"

Richard wanted to ignore that question, but he decided to throw a challenge to the reporter instead. He sometimes did that to incite their curiosity.

He had worked hard to build a multi-billion- dollar company. He believed that with hard work and determination anyone could be as successful as him.

He paused a moment, turned to the reporter and said, "You would agree with me that there wouldn't be much fun in your reporting if I were to give you all of the answers now, wouldn't you? Find out what was the nature of my visit to Liberia. I'm sure you will feel more accomplished doing so than if I were to tell you."

Having issued that challenge, he ignored other questions as he exited the terminal and inhaled deeply. The weather reminded him of the warm sunny days in Liberia, but it was much welcomed because he was back in LA. He was glad he had made the trip and felt justified in his accomplishment.

"Good afternoon, Martin," he greeted his chauffeur who held the door open for him.

"Welcome back Mr. Mcgallan. I trust your trip went well?"

"Very well indeed, Martin. Thanks for asking."

Martin, his very trusted and committed chauffeur, had worked for him for nearly eleven years. When it came to his itineraries and activities, Martin had rights to full disclosure.

Ensuring that Richard was comfortably seated in the limousine, Martin shut the door then he returned to his seat and drove away.

Richard relaxed for the drive to his home, Palmridge Haven. His five-tower mansion, perched on a hilltop, accented the skyline of the nearby beach. It was the zenith of a rolling landscape covering about twelve acres of land. Palmridge was his retreat, offering the comfort and serenity which steered his determination to be successful in business.

Richard felt re-energized hours later by the time he entered his home office. He sat at his desk going through the schedule and notes which Marilyn had arranged for him when his phone rang.

The ring tone and the caller ID indicated it was Shannon, his "on and off" girlfriend. He had not seen her since she mentioned the "M" word, which in his highly sophisticated vocabulary was synonymous to "affair's over." Marriage was a sacrifice as far as he knew, and he'd rather pass than take the plunge.

He would have to assign the task of ending the affair to Marilyn, his efficient secretary. He had no doubt she would inform Shannon in the most subtle way possible.

He assured himself that this would be the final break-up. He felt it would be heartless to continue seeing her since he could never give her what she wanted most from him. So, this time, his end-of-affair gift would have to be very substantial. Richard thought of it as an "unofficial alimony" for years of being with him.

He sent her call to his voicemail and glanced at his watch in anticipation of Terry's arrival. He needed to know about the status of the finances of Weisener Enterprise. It was more important than talking with Shannon.

Muffled voices and then a knock on the door announced his brother's arrival.

"Welcome back, Rich," Terry said, walking over to give his brother a hug.

"Thanks. It's good to be back."

Scrutinizing Richard with concerned brown eyes he said, "I suppose there's no need to inquire on your health because you look very well. I mean... considering you needed to get a greenlight from your doctor before you made another donation."

"If I felt any better than this, I'd be a meta-human."

Terry chuckled and Richard smiled.

Richard was one of twenty people in the world who could donate the "golden blood" Rh_{null}. A little boy in Liberia needed blood transfusion and the protocol necessary for transporting blood across countries would not allow the child to get the transfusion soon enough. He had taken the resources at his disposal and flown over in his private jet to donate his blood.

Richard had left the country before his doctor's clearance that it was safe to make another donation. He had donated blood less than four weeks prior to making the trip. His doctor had insisted on running tests before he could give Richard his consent for another donation. But Richard felt he would be okay, so he had traveled to donate the "golden blood."

He had become immune to Terry's routine scrutiny of him whenever he returned from such trips. In fact, he had expected his younger brother would have tried to play doctor when he arrived.

"Well, let's get to business," Richard told Terry. "What are the details on Weisener Enterprise's financial status and the progress of the merger? Are we going to be losing in this merger?"

The proposed merger from the owner of Weisener Enterprise was unexpected. They had longed to purchase the company for such a long time that the offer seemed almost too good to be true.

"Actually, the books looked really good. Which makes his offer of a merger even more mind boggling," Terry replied.

Terry was the CFO of the company. When it came to financial analysis, Richard had yet to meet another person as skilled as his brother.

"I'm glad to know, it's not going to be a money pit. How did the meeting with the team go?"

"That's one tough group but I'd have to say the meeting went well."

"Tough group—meaning?"

"Some interesting questions and comments brought forth."

"Well that's expected since they're probably feeling unsure about imminent changes, isn't it?"

"It is but a member of the team taking a jab at you was totally unexpected."

That resulted in a raised brow, "I'm listening..."

Terry looked at his brother and replied, "She said she had her reservations about you as CEO of the company but hearing that you go around the world helping people, she stands corrected."

She had made the comment when Terry had explained that Richard could not be at the meeting because he had gone to be of assistance in another country.

Richard understood it for what it was—sarcasm. His gaze narrowed and a frown creased his forehead. It was one thing to experience resistance from new employees, but he did not tolerate impertinence from his employees.

"Who is she and what's her position at the company?"

"Her name is Elvira Whitman and she is a corporate counselor, Rich. She rose to the top by defeating a team of elite corporate lawyers right out of college. She is held in high esteem among her colleagues from what I understand."

Richard sipped his wine, "Well then one of our newly acquired legal departments could certainly use her expertise."

Richard paused before asking, "Now, what else do I need to know?"

"What makes you think there's more to say?"

"As I always say, you have to work on that poker face of yours. It's not convincing."

Terry smiled and turned to look out the floor to ceiling glass door. Richard did not need to know about Emeline, the woman he could not get off his mind. That was *his* problem, not Richard's. But he knew Richard would not stop asking unless he came up with a suitable response.

He sipped his drink, "The meeting started about ten minutes after the scheduled time. You might want to reiterate the need for timeliness at the company."

That was a non-negotiable policy at his company, "They arrived *that* late?"

"One of them, Weisener's granddaughter, Emeline."

Okay, so this was the piece of information he had been withholding, Richard thought.

He stared at his brother, "I'd like to assume she's beautiful?"

Terry rubbed his eyes as if to erase any traces of her image from his eyes, "Very beautiful."

"And...?"

"And she is very brilliant but thinks the world revolves around her."

"Something tells me you are interested?"

"Sorry, not my type," Terry replied fiercely.

"Right..."

But Richard wanted nothing to influence Terry's decisions on the merger in progress. He knew his brother could go to extreme lengths once he set his mind on pursuing a woman. Fortunately, the business had not been compromised as a result of that.

"She won't be a distraction when it comes to making financial decisions, will she?" Richard asked.

"Trust me when I say, there is close to zero chance of that happening?"

"That's a relief."

"She's off my radar, Rich. Besides, as far as my taste for women goes, I'd say she's definitely bitter pills, not my usual sweet soft caramel candy kind."

"Uh...huh," was all Richard got in then the door opened, and their mother walked in.

Chapter Two

Vivi walked into the grand entry way of the Falcon Nest wearing a burgundy sleeveless satin gown. The V-necked crystals beaded front emphasized her tiny waistline, making her a showstopper.

What am I doing here again? she wondered for the tenth time. Her friend Emeline Weisener had received the invitation to the ball in the mail but had said she had no plans for attending. It was a masquerade ball hosted by Mcgallan Foundations.

"I'll go in your place," Vivi had informed her.

"Really?"

"Of course."

"Good. At least the invitation won't go to waste. Terrance Mcgallan and I should stay miles apart whenever possible."

Vivi had accepted the invitation, thinking this was a first for Emmy—refusing to go to a ball. Emmy was a social butterfly and enjoyed partying. So, she never seemed to lack invitations to different events. This time the invitation was sent by a friend of hers who was catering at the ball.

Vivi made the trip from San Francisco to LA but she felt justified in doing so. She wanted to see the new CEO in action on another turf.

A masquerade ball was perfect since it would conceal her identity, but it brought back so much memories. She remembered the last time she was at a masquerade ball. She had been so naïve then. If only she could turn back the clock. Taking in a deep breath, she made her way into the ballroom of the five-star hotel.

Blending in with the rest of the guests in the crowded room, she saw clustered groups of ladies. A closer look suggested the Mcgallan brothers were probably the center of attraction for these groups. She could not be sure but as she stepped closer, she heard another male guest call out "hey Richard" and he returned his friend's greetings.

Richard Mcgallan looked suave and sharp in a blue cocktail suit. She noticed women overtly contending for his attention.

One of them leaned closer and whispered to him then walked away. Vivi rolled her eyes in exasperation when he chuckled in response. He turned his head in her direction at that exact moment and eyes as dark as the mid-night clouds pierced hers beneath the mask. He had seen her eye roll and was instantly intrigued.

His eyes followed her as she wove her way through the crowd. There was something peculiarly familiar about her. Why did he feel like he had met her before, even though her face was hidden by the mask?

"On behalf of my family, I would like to thank all of you for attending this charity ball tonight," Richard began.

His eyes searched the room for the stunning challenger he had seen earlier as he gave the welcome speech. Her eyes had become dismissive then swept nonchalantly over him before she turned her back to weave her way towards the hors d'oeuvre. It was as if she had spoken "you are not worth my time" loud and clear to him. Did she know he was all game to meet that challenge?

He saw her heading towards the doorway as he continued, "We hope you have fun and contribute generously to a worthy cause."

When he got off the stage, he saw her exit the room as the music began. It was time to meet this mysterious yet familiar woman, he told himself.

Vivi sat on a bench in the garden enjoying the crisp cool breeze of the night. Her brief encounter with Richard had been unsettling so she had exited the ballroom, making her way outside. She had intended to return shortly but the serenity of the view before her had beckoned to her.

She stared at the beach observing there was no one else in sight. What a great location she thought–a hotel with a beach in its backyard. Closing her eyes, she inhaled the sweet-smelling fragrances of the night. She smiled and leaned her head back.

"A gorgeous serene night, isn't it?"

Vivi was startled because she had not heard footsteps approaching but she managed to conceal her surprise. After all what kind of lawyer would she be if she were ruffled by the deep baritone of the man she had left speaking at the ball?

"It is, which makes your intrusion very much unwelcomed."

"Touché."

Too bad, he thought, because you just got company.

"There appears to be enough room for one more."

He gestured to the bench upon which she sat. "Is that seat taken?" He asked, taking a seat before she could respond.

"Why bother asking anyway when you didn't intend to wait for my response, Richard?"

Richard reached up and removed his mask, "I don't believe wearing this makes any difference anymore since you already know who I am."

"Don't expect me to remove my mask also."

"Then I'm at a disadvantage here. So, who do I have the pleasure of speaking to?" Richard asked hoping she would not refuse to tell him.

Vivi pondered on his question for a moment. She did not intend on giving him her full name, but she thought her nickname would suffice under the circumstances.

"Vivi," she replied.

"Is that short for Vivian?"

"Sort of."

Richard wanted to inquire on that response, but he decided against it.

"Tired already with the pretty little women chasing after you."

"I'm an alpha male, Vivi."

She could tell what he was hinting at, but she asked, "Meaning?"

He shrugged, "In a game, the alpha male cannot be chased as a prey."

"I don't play games," she told him, reaching nervously for the locket on her neck. His eyes were drawn to her fingers which he thought were uniquely beautiful. He also noticed her elegant digital wristwatch.

Richard slid his arm over the backrest and turned slightly towards her, legs crossed. He was close enough that his breath fanned her cheek, warming and caressing it.

"That is why I'm not sure if you made a wise choice coming out here alone."

Certainly, she knew he would have come in search of her after that very intense non-verbal exchange.

She responded, "What could possibly be wrong about sitting alone near the beach in this scenic garden?"

"Well for one thing there could be sharks lurking somewhere on the beach," he joked.

He leaned closer and his hand on the headrest reached out to lightly brush back stray hair. Maybe it was time she abandoned her operation here, she thought.

"Do you mean the sharks that inhabit the ocean or the ones that roam the land?"

"I wasn't aware there were sharks roaming the land."

"Perhaps that's because it's your school."

He threw back his head and laughed, making her aware of his sense of humor. She cautioned herself to be mindful as the stern lines on his face relaxed making him amiable.

Richard lifted a lock of her hair and watched her closely as he let it fall. It was light and felt like silk between his fingers.

Butterflies fluttered deep within her stomach flaring up torrents of warm coziness cascading like a waterfall. She felt the awakening of sensations left dormant for far to long.

"And what do the sharks that roam the land prey on?" he said huskily.

"You tell *me*. It's your school of fish."

"Pursue steamy, hot ladies with impressively beautiful legs, perhaps?" he responded.

Then he kissed her softly, pulling her closer with the hand which was on the headrest while his other hand roamed her legs visible below her dress.

She hesitated for couple of seconds, knowing that making out with him was playing with fire. But a voice deep within her nudged her on so she kissed him back. His clean spicy scent overshadowed the fragrance from the flowers heightening her response. She would reject his advances soon, in a minute, but after... She moaned with pleasure then his lips left hers.

Richard stood up and extended his hand. She looked up at him, confused and still dazed by the kiss.

"Trust me," he whispered hoarsely.

She took his hand realizing that the gesture affirmed she trusted him. They walked through the garden then went pass a fountain glimmering in the moonlight.

He led her through a hidden door and into a suite with state-of-the-art décor. The carpet was plush and sank deep beneath her feet. In the middle of the room was a table set for two with fruits, crackers, cheese, and wine on ice. Richard poured wine in two glasses and gave her one.

She sipped the wine, enjoying the warm fiery taste. Was she setting herself up to be burned by this man who took whatever he wanted whenever he could get it? She questioned her decision to be alone with him, in his lair of all places.

He seemed to have intentionally planned to bring someone to his suite.

"Well planned. A table for two all laid out," she said nodding towards the table.

He shrugged, "I assure you this was done with no other woman but you on my mind."

Did he assume she would have been that easy to persuade like the women of his circle? She had proven him right, hadn't she? After all, she *was* alone with him just as he had intended.

"So, did you think I would be an easy target?"

"No, I didn't, but I thought you were an enticing challenge to pursue. But then that was your intention wasn't it...to entice me?"

She looked at him with such incredulity that he chuckled. "I'm just kidding. That look you gave me at the ball was clearly a warning to back off if I've ever seen one."

She smiled. So, he had gotten her message. How astute, he understood body language. He wouldn't have gotten far in the business world without such skills.

"Are you hungry," he asked, "because I'm starving so how about you relax and let's eat?"

Her stomach rumbled silently reminding her it was long past her dinner time so she did not argue.

He led her to a sofa and sat next to her. Her senses went on high alert, especially when she thought about the scene in the garden. She said nothing but her eyes spoke volume.

Richard felt her nervousness when his leg brushed hers inadvertently. Dark brown eyes stared into hazel brown ones. Certainly, she knew he wanted more than just dinner and polite chatter?

She broke eye contact with him and reached for some grapes. Aware that he was still staring, she ate the grapes avoiding his eyes.

"I noticed you came in alone; where is your plus one?"

"I'm here on a work-related assignment."

His gaze narrowed. She was not a reporter, was she? He'd had multiple encounters with female reporters who tried to advance their careers at his expense.

"Oh..., so your profession is ...?"

"Let's just say I help people make the right decisions and help them out when they encounter obstacles."

That response only stirred up more questions. She was being evasive but at least it did not match the job description of a reporter. Unless... it was probably a cover-up? He would have to be careful.

Rather than take her back to the ballroom as it was the logical thing to have done, he said to her, "Try the strawberries. They're good."

She stared at his hand holding the fruit to her mouth. Okay, this was getting more intimate by the minute. But she was held mesmerized by the same force that had so magnetically propelled her in his lair.

"Here, have a bite," his voice appeared to have dropped an octave.

She obeyed biting half of the fruit. Then she watched as he ate the other half. He held her gaze as he did so and she shivered at the intimacy.

Hoping to diffuse the tension, Vivi forced her eyes away and reached for some crackers. They ate in silence for a while. Then with the flick of a button, MKTO-Classic filled the room.

Before he went out into the garden to find her, Richard had selected that music. He did so because when he first saw her in the ballroom the word "classic" had come to mind.

He pulled her to her feet and into his arms. "Since we are here for the ball, I figured I could at least have one dance with you."

"So... let me guess, next, I will receive a hefty dose of seduction?"

In response to her question he lowered his head and brushed his lips against hers. Her lips were sweet with the lingering taste of the strawberries. He pulled her closer and felt her heartbeat against his chest.

The fragrance she wore was exotic causing him to inhale deeply. It was a blend of lilac, which he had first assumed was from the garden, and another fragrance he couldn't quite tell, jasmine, or lavender?

One hand reached up to gently rub the tip of her breast. She moaned as her nipple hardened against his touch. Was it her imagination or did his touch feel familiar? She trembled with excitement and reached out to trace his jawline then her hand curled around his neck. The kiss deepened as he explored the warmth of her mouth hungrily. Then she was lifted off her feet and carried gently in his arms.

Where was he taking her? What was she thinking? Hadn't she learned her lesson? She could not give in to the yearnings of her body.

"No," she said.

He became still and let her slide to her feet promptly. As he sought to steady his spiraling emotions, he asked, "Why?"

"I'm sorry, I can't do this.

"Why?" he asked again.

"I'll just say I've been down this path before and it's not one I'd want to take again," she replied reaching for her locket again in a way that was becoming familiar.

"Could you at least be more specific?"

"Figure it out. I'm not going to spell it out for you," she replied hurrying towards the door.

"Wait," Richard called out to her. She stopped and turned around as he caught up with her in few strides.

He rubbed his head, "Sorry, you were right to stop me. I moved too fast considering we just met."

It was a sincere apology, but she made no comment, just met his gaze. She was to blame also because she had encouraged it in a way, wasn't she?

He gave her a black and gold card, "I thought you should have this... my number."

Vivi took it from him and stared at the number wondering why he could not ask for her number instead, if he really wanted to keep in touch with her? Not that she would have given her number to him but at least he would have made the attempt to ask for it.

Vivi took out her phone and looking at the card, she typed in some numbers. She noticed his phone lying on the table where he'd put it when they entered the suite.

Assuming she was storing his number, he said to her "Promise me that you will call."

Vivi looked him in the eye, "I already did but it is not your number is it?"

"No, it is my office line," he confessed.

"Meaning it is the number for your secretary whose job is to filter your calls? Am I supposed to wait in a queue?" What number am I on the list, anyway?"

She was right, Richard thought. He could have given her his direct line but as a rule he never gave his direct line to a woman until after the third date. By then he usually had a report from his private detective on the woman.

He said to Vivi, "I promise, your call will be forwarded to me immediately. You won't have to wait."

When she made no comment but simply stared at him, he said "Please don't let this be the only time we spent together, Vivi."

"Oh, I'm sure we will be spending some time together, one way or another, Richard."

She turned and walked away, leaving him perplexed. She made a mental note to toss the card into the nearest trash bin as soon as she possibly could. She would not be calling him.

Richard watched her leave. He wanted to get one of his security to follow her, but that would be stalking, wouldn't it? Like the other women he knew, he assumed she would call him and if she didn't call him, then he would have to seek his private detective's help. One problem though—he only knew her nickname, but she *had* called his office line, hadn't she? He would just have to get his office phone records for the night and Bob would get him the information he needed about her.

Chapter Three

Three weeks later, Richard stopped at his secretary's desk to inquire, "Any new calls for me, Marilyn?"

"Couple of them, sir. The names and contact information are on your desk as always, Mr. Mcgallan."

His secretary stared after him in disbelieve. For once he didn't seem in control of something. He was asking about a call from the woman she was fast becoming a fan of, referring to her as "Mrs. Right." He had given Marilyn instructions to clear up his schedule when she called.

She smiled and even though she had yet to see or hear from this mysterious woman, Marilyn felt it was about time he met a woman with a mind of her own—a woman who did not dance to the tune of his guitar strings.

Richard had waited patiently for Vivi to call him but she hadn't. The silence and wait had been unbearable. Fortunately, the merger with Weisener Enterprise had kept him busy.

It was going on as planned and now he was stationed at Weisener Enterprise for a while until he had met with all employees. That way he could also make sure other processes that reflected his company's values were in full swing at the newly merged company.

Every day he longed for her. Her honey-colored skin was soft and warm to his touch. The taste of her lips still lingered on his, every waking moment. Would she call him at all? He could wait no longer. He picked up his phone and made some calls.

One call was made to his private detective who began working right away on Richard's request. Marilyn faxed over requested information to the private detective.

Why did Vivi preoccupy his thoughts so much? Richard wondered. It was the first time in years that he had not thought about his escapade at another masquerade ball.

Could he ever forget Spitfire? He had met and had a one-night affair with her at a masquerade ball on a resort in the Caribbean. She had left while he was asleep and inquiries made on her had been fruitless.

He had visited the resort every year since that time, even purchased the resort, but he had not found her. He had never stopped trying to find her until now. What if he did not find Vivi also? He could not allow that to happen again. He opened his computer and engrossed himself in his work.

Days later, Richard's investigator had no favorable leads for him. Even the office caller ID gave no clues. Who was this woman who had covered her tracks with such precision?

Vivi reread the email she had received from Marilyn. She had an appointment scheduled to meet Richard. He had been meeting with the employees and she would be his last appointment for the day.

He had been working from the CEO's office on the third floor at Weisener Enterprise for few days now.

She was glad the office was large enough so she did not run into Richard as she had feared but the moment of truth had arrived. Why was she his last appointment for the day? Did he suspect or realize that she was the woman he had met at the ball?

She walked into his secretary's office promptly. "Mr. Mcgallan your last appointment is here." Marilyn told him on the telephone.

Richard raised his head from a pile of papers before him to reply to his secretary. He was looking at the guest list from the fundraising ball and his office phone records from that night. What he did not know was that Vivi had blocked her number when she made the call that night so Bob had not found her. Richard had decided to hire another detective and he wanted to provide the new guy with substantial information. He thought there *had* to be some clues the lists could offer.

"Thanks, Marilyn. Please sent her in," he said to his secretary then went back to browsing the list.

"Mr. Mcgallan will see you now, Ms. Whitman," Marilyn replied looking at the name on the appointment.

Vivi walked into the room bracing herself for the encounter. She was relieved to find that he was browsing over some papers spread out on his desk. It would give her some time to gather up her poise.

"Please have a seat, Ms. Whitman," Richard told her without even raising his head from the papers.

Interesting, she thought. He must really be trying to meet some deadline on a new project, she supposed. Or perhaps he was being condescending?

Richard had not forgotten about the sarcastic remark made by Elvira Whitman when he had traveled to Africa. The plan was to make her sit and wait for a while before he consulted with her on her position at the company. It was his way of letting her know that he demanded nothing but ultimate respect from his employees.

Vivi took advantage of this time to stare at him. His hard jawlines, which emphasized his determination to be successful, were chiseled. His lips, she had to admit, were perfectly shaped and pleasurable. She could not resist taking in sharp breath silently as she recalled the kisses they shared. Then her eyes roamed over his face now creased in concentration as he as perused the papers before him. She watched his muscles flex as he moved the papers around. How much time did he spend at the gym? He was buffed. Her eyes returned to his lips, reliving their night together.

Richard could sense her eyes on him, although he tried to focus on the papers before him. Why was his body responding to the stare of a woman he had not even met?

Closing the papers before him he pulled open the manila folder marked Elvira Whitman and browsed the information as he readied to talk to her.

"Thanks for waiting Ms. Whitman," he said raising his head to look at her.

His brows furrowed in confusion. He saw Vivi in the woman sitting in his office. It seemed like his obsession to find her was having more effect on him then he thought.

Vivi reached nervously for the locket resting against her chest. Richard's gaze narrowed as he remembered vividly how one other woman had reached for a similar locket weeks ago at the masquerade ball. Those gorgeous fingers, the wristwatch, and her mannerism of reaching for her locket was a dead giveaway. Elvira Whitman *had* to be Vivi.

Stunned, he stood to his feet, "Vivi?"

"I think you have me mistaken for someone else," she lied.

"Then is it a coincidence that Vivi, a lady I met at a masquerade ball, has the same locket and wristwatch as yours? I'm no fool Elvira," he said calmly.

He had not referred to her fingers because he was not going to compliment her knowing she had deceived him.

"How long did you think you could have carried on this charade?"

She could not deny that she was wearing her locket even if she could deny wearing the identical wristwatch.

"Okay, so it was me at the ball. What are you going to do about that?"

What really did she want from him? First the sarcastic remark then a charade? She must certainly be up to something.

He replied, "I'm thinking about it."

Vivi stood up gracefully, "Good, my appointment with you was scheduled for today but perhaps it is best to reschedule our meeting for another day. I'm sure you would have had it all figured out by then."

She turned to leave when he called out, "Don't even think about leaving this room, Elvira."

Despite his firm tone, she liked the sound of her name on his lips. She felt quivers cruising down her spine but dismissed the feeling as nervousness.

"Have a seat," he told her.

Vivi sat down in the chair. After all he was her boss and she was a stellar employee so she would show him respect in that capacity even if he were behaving like an intolerable jerk.

Richard took his seat and glanced at her folder a moment. It was then that he realized her middle name was Vivian.

He said to her, "Tell me about yourself, Elvira."

She went into a repertoire about her professional life. If he wanted details about her private life, he would not be getting it, she told herself.

Richard listened to her patiently, all the time thinking about the adjustment he would have to make to his relationship policy. He had never gone against his "no-employee rule" before but then he had met her at a masquerade ball. Had he not? So technically he would not be going against his rule, would he?

When she stopped speaking, he held her gaze, "Am I right in assuming you are single?"

There was no wedding band so he was hopeful that she was not already taken but he needed to hear her say it. He did not care if there was a fiancé or boyfriend.

Vivi replied, "The last time I checked that topic fell under the label "private life" and I'd prefer to keep it tucked privately away from my work life."

He nodded. "Good, which means you are available to accompany me whenever..."

Absolutely not. She would not give him reason to think she was available, not for him anyway.

She replied, "No husband but, I *am* in a committed relationship."

He did not take that information well. An image of her kissing someone else flashed before his eyes, igniting his primitive instinct. Anger stiffened the muscles at his neck. He was not sure whether he was angry at her, or her boyfriend, or himself for being attracted to her.

"I bet your boyfriend is not aware of our dirty little secret from weeks ago?" He heard himself ask, regretting it the moment the words were out.

Vivi stared at him for what seemed like a minute, not speaking. He returned her gaze unwaveringly. Did he really try to come at her like that?

She responded, "He is aware that as part of my job sometimes I have to conduct fact-finding investigations. Last week escapade, rightly so, qualifies as one of such inquiries so, he will have no problem with that. But I'd have to say the result was in line with my assumption."

She saw the twitching at his jawline and knew she had scored. Realizing now was probably the best time to make her exit, she stood up.

Smiling sweetly at him she asked, "Surely, you didn't think I had fallen for your charm, did you? I would hate to spell this out for you bluntly, but I will not be one of those women satisfying your lust, Richard Mcgallan.

Richard leaned back in his chair smiling dangerously, "You shouldn't have said that Elvira. The moment you uttered those words, it was a done deal. You will satisfy my lust— your words not mine— and I will make sure that *you* beg *me* to do that before I leave here to return to my head office."

"Then you will have to return to your head office very much unsatisfied."

Richard replied, "We'll see about that."

"Now that we're clear on that, I'd have to say this meeting with you is over," Vivi told him, standing to leave.

Richard moved with lightning speed. He was on his feet and around the desk, facing her, before she could even take a step.

"No, Elvira. That is my call to decide when or if this meeting is over, not yours."

He was close, too close for her to maintain her cool and reason was evading her. She backed away until she was sandwiched between the desk and him.

Richard murmured throatily, "As far as I can see, this meeting has just begun."

The tension in the room shifted from anger to sexual awareness as they faced off. Silently Vivi and Richard engaged in a battle of desire.

"Do I make myself clear, Elvira?" he asked. He was so close that she felt his groin against her.

Unable to speak or control her racing heart, she nodded. She watched as his hand shot out to pull her ponytail loose. She never wore her hair down at work.

He inhaled sharply as her hair came loose. He combed his fingers through it, and then his hand traveled to the pulse beating eagerly at the base of her neck.

"So... did you get all the data you needed for your fact-finding investigation?" he murmured before his lips descended on hers.

Vivi did not have the chance to reply or protest verbally. So she opted for being passive. She did not kiss him back, but Richard felt her body betray her as it responded to his every touch. One hand traveled down the neckline of the business suit and rested lightly on her pounding heart. Then just as the vaporized aroma of an essential oil on a burner infuses a room, the smell of jasmine permeated his office. Her perfume, he smiled knowingly. It was only a matter of time before her mind give in as well.

He reached for the locket lying between her breasts. Holding her gaze, he held the heart-shaped pendent in his hand. He had a feeling it was incredibly special to her as he brought the pendant to his lips.

Letting go of the pendant his mouth teased hers, cajoling her with unswerving persuasion. The caresses from his hands and mouth chipped away her resolve to remain impassive as her true emotions were unveiled. When he palmed her breast, she whimpered softly. It was her breaking point and her hands, which were resting stubbornly on the desk, went around his neck.

She returned his kisses, accepting the emotions assailing her. Her legs buckled and he lifted her onto his desk. She moaned when he unbuttoned her top, exploring what he had craved since that night. They were more enticing then he had imagined and as sweet as pears. He shivered with excitement. These belonged to him now so it was hands or eyes off to any other man. And that boyfriend she claimed to have, he would make sure the guy was ousted.

Her whimpers echoed around them in the room and his mouth found hers again. He shuddered, longing for more but the office was not the place.

His mouth left hers and his hands came to rest on the desk on both sides of her hips. Breathing heavily, he gripped the desk as he sought to steady the passion consuming him.

Vivi opened her eyes to see his emotion glazed eyes staring into hers accusingly. She realized she should have kept her resolve to be unresponsive to him all along. He was only trying to disprove her previous claim.

"So...can we both agree to toss the fact-finding claim out the window?" he asked huskily.

She closed her eyes but did not respond to his question. Willing herself to get a grip on her emotions, she inhaled slowly. Hadn't she known this was his intention?

"You heard me, Elvira. What's your defense for responding to me this time?"

When she opened her eyes she replied, "So I guess we're even. You played your cards well. It must be a big deal for you when it comes to me."

Releasing the desk, he stood tall, "We're not even, Elvira. A draw or loss results in a status change of the alpha-male so losing or drawing in a game is not an option for me."

His finger trailed a path along her jawline to her lips, "Be warned, Elvira, you started this game and I intend to finish it. If there will be a loser here it won't be me."

She turned away from him as she fastened her top then turning to face him she squared her shoulders and replied, "Perhaps I should remind you that technically, this is our second time meeting and you can't claim to have won the first time, can you?"

She smiled when he made no response. "I thought so." Then she turned around and walked towards the door.

Richard stared after her. She was right, he thought. She *had* won the first time. He had almost lost his sanity trying to find her but he won't admit that.

As she approached the door he called out, "Elvira."

She turned around wondering what he had to say this time. "Richard."

"Three is definitely a crowd so open relationship is not my thing. That means someone has to go and as a rule, the alpha male always stays. As you may have noticed, I'm very proprietary."

"You must be out of your mind."

"The fact that you're being told suggests quite the contrary."

"Mr. Mcgallan, in case you don't know this, the only request you can ask of me is work related and nothing else." With that she stormed out of his office slamming the door behind her.

Marilyn Skinner stared after Vivi wondering what might have happened behind those closed doors. She noticed Vivi's hair hung loose on her shoulders which was different from earlier. Then she remembered a coworker had called Elvira, "Vivi." A light bulb went up and she smiled. Had Mr. Mcgallan finally found Vivi? At least he knew where to look if he did not get his "call."

Chapter Four

Richard stared at the closed door for a while then he sat at his desk and dialed Bob. Before he got too involved, he needed to know more about her.

He provided the information Bob needed. With the detective's expertise, he might uncover whatever dirt was hidden.

"So I take it you were able to get in touch with Vivi after all?" his private detective asked.

"Yes," he replied.

He was still puzzled that he had not seen her in the building since he'd taken office at the company. He had gone through her department on his tour of the office so was she out that day or did she just try to avoid him?

Vivi was a challenge but didn't he like challenges? She was a unique challenge which came with many benefits. He smiled when he thought about how she had tried to take control by telling *him* the meeting was over. He should be mad about that but he had not had a more stimulating conversation with a woman since he became a billionaire. Every woman he met since that time had danced to the tune he played so this was refreshing.

He glanced at his watch then messaged his lead security, William, to have Martin bring his car around. It was heads-up to his security detail.

Richard left the office surrounded by his bodyguards who had discreetly roamed the floor on which his office was situated. One of his men held the door open for him when he reached the car. As he was about to enter his limousine, he saw his lead security talking to a woman in a car. It was none other than Elvira. Jealous rage was the only description that matched the emotions he felt.

William was not the other guy in Vivi's life, was he? He wondered. He walked over to them hoping there was a good explanation for what appeared to be a flirty encounter.

As he got closer, he saw William go around and open the hood of the car while Vivi started the car. He let out a sigh of relief. William was probably helping Vivi.

Richard walked to where William stood and asked, "What's going on?"

"I think it's the fan belt," William replied. "Those need changing after about sixty thousand miles. She'll have to call for a ride and a tow truck."

Richard needed assurance that there was no past, present or future connections between Vivi and his lead security. "Is she a friend of yours?"

"No, we just met. I walked over when her car made that screeching noise. Now I have to tell her the bad news."

"I will give her a ride home and I'll talk with her about her car," he told William.

Vivi sat in the car waiting to hear what the problem with her car might be. Her day had started well but since her meeting with Richard Mcgallan, it seemed as if everything was going south.

When she had left his office, she'd raced to hers then left hurriedly hoping to leave the building so that she did not encounter him on her way out. The worse that could have happened was to ride the same elevator with him. She had sped to the elevator then to the parking lot.

She had commended herself on avoiding further contact with him as she drove past the front entrance of the building. Then she had heard her car make an unfamiliar sound. She was the first owner of the car and it had less than seventy miles on it. She serviced it regularly so why would it have problem now?

Vivi heard the hood snap shut and tensed when she saw Richard standing next to the man who had come to her aid. She watched them walk over then Richard leaned over the window to talk to her.

"Elvira, your car needs to be towed so I will give you a ride home," Richard said.

"Thanks, but that won't be necessary. I will call for a ride."

She was not going to ride the car with him, she told herself. Vivi reached for her cellphone and browsed her contacts.

Realizing it would be difficult getting her to accept a ride from him he turned to William who had never thought he would ever see a woman reject Richard's offer.

"William, could you go to make the arrangements to have Ms. Whitman's car towed away, please?"

William took out his phone and walked away, giving them privacy. His boss didn't need to say it twice, it was obvious there was some chemistry between the boss and the woman he was calling Elvira.

When William turned away and was out of earshot, Richard reached for her phone. Snatching it from her hands, he ended her attempt to call for a ride.

"You will not contact him in my presence, Elvira."

"Who do you know I'm calling?"

"Your boyfriend?"

Was he that jealous? "It's really none of your business. I need my phone, please."

"You will get your phone as soon as you are in the limousine. Now, you have two choices, you can walk to the limo, or I can carry you.

He opened the door to her car, "You have five seconds to get out."

He couldn't be serious, could he? He was not really going to follow through on that threat, or was he? She glanced up at him and had the chilling feeling that he was not bluffing. Vivi needed to maintain her professional reputation among her colleagues so she chose to gracefully get out of the car.

As he walked by her side on their way to his limo, Richard said "Your car keys, please."

She stared at him not sure why he wanted her keys and he went on to explain, "The mechanic will need that to work on your car."

She took out her keys and a business card, "That's the name and contact information of my mechanic." Then she added, "Thanks."

"You are welcome," he replied but he did not inform her that her car would be going to the company's mechanic.

Vivi sat in the limousine, in no mood to converse with Richard because he had been haughty. When he slid next to her in the limousine, she inched away to avoid any physical contact with him.

Keeping his distance Richard turned to give her what appeared to be a tablet.

"Enter your address, Elvira, unless you won't mind having dinner with me tonight?"

Taking the device from him, she typed in her address. She realized the limousine had a custom-built GPS as the car began to move in the direction of her home. Was the GPS audible to the driver? She wondered since it was inaudible on their end. However, the route to her home was visible on the device which he had replaced on its stand.

Richard returned her phone once they were on their way. Then he heard the notification alert on his own phone. Pleased to have it as a distraction, he browsed through the notifications. There was an email from Bob so he perused that quickly.

He glanced over at Vivi who was engrossed in her phone. The report from Bob indicated that she was from a small town in North Carolina, and she had not visited the town for about ten years. She had no siblings and her parents still lived there. It seemed strange that she had not gone to see them. It appeared they had indulged her and she loved them but then she disappeared suddenly and never returned. There was definitely a reason why she had stayed away for such a long time.

"So...it must be hard staying away from your hometown this long. Ten years is a very long time, if you ask me."

Vivi raised her head sharply, not sure how he had gotten that information.

"What did you say?"

"It must be difficult for your parents...you've been away for such a long time. Or do your parents come to visit you instead?

"I certainly did not disclose such private detail of my life in my resume so how do you know that?"

"It is the digital age so it is really easy to get information about a person of interest. I have my ways of doing just that."

She was indignant, "What did you do, Richard?"

He shrugged, "Not me. I had my private investigator do his job. I had to know about you before we went further."

"Who says I'm going any further with you?"

"I did and I know you want to too. At least so your body tells me."

"Then you must have a very active imagination."

He reached for her chin and tipped her head so that he was looking her in the eyes, "Do you deny that you don't want to know where this chemistry between us will lead?"

It would be a lie if she said no and he would think she was interested in him if she said otherwise. So she replied, "Believe what you want."

He let her go, "I thought so. The pastor's daughter cannot tell a lie, can she?"

If only he knew the lie she was living, "Remember, no one is perfect. At least I don't claim to be."

"Hmm, now that's what I call honesty."

She was seething with anger. What did the investigator uncover besides the question he was asking? Perhaps Richard knowing about her past was to her benefit after all. He would certainly run the other way if he discovered the skeletons in her closet. So why was she not excited about him abandoning the chase?

"Well, hopefully your curiosity or rather obsession with my private life has been satisfied by that report."

He wanted to tell her his obsession with her had yet to be satisfied but instead he said, "Actually, I believe if you will just answer my previous question I'll have all the information I need for now."

"You mean after what you spent to get the information you still have a missing piece of the puzzle? So much for being a billionaire. How much did you pay the guy again?"

He chuckled, "*That* I'm not telling you."

The limo reached her building and came to a stop. She rushed out of the limousine. He went after her and walked her to the entry way. He brushed her cheeks lightly then waited as she went into the building before he went back to the limo. Vivi watched him go then slowly raised her hand to her neck and touched the charm that held the answer to the question he asked.

Chapter Five

Vivi called Emmy to ask for a ride to work because her car was at the mechanic shop. Emmy was always running late but she was the best option at the moment. She hoped her car would be done before the end of the workday. A text message informed her Emmy had arrived. She was glad her friend was on time.

"Thanks for the ride on a last-minute notice, Emmy. I honestly thought I would have had to wait much longer."

Both women giggled knowing the implication of her last statement.

"I'm aware that you believe in punctuality so I have to get you there on time."

"That's very thoughtful of you, thanks."

"No problem, I always enjoy carpooling with you."

Elvira was her best friend and a sister figure. Girls night out with Vivi was one of her favorite past-time.

Emmy glanced over at Vivi, "So, talk to me about our new boss?"

"I'll sum it up in three words—obnoxious, egotistical, and infuriating."

"Hmmm...Wrong description for a man I think is amusing, eye-catching and amiably charming."

Vivi shrugged, "Ironically speaking, *your* description would work."

Emmy smiled. She knew about Vivi's aversion for the rich and powerful but she could sense there was definitely something going on.

"Now your description may well apply to his brother."

"I don't know... Terry strikes me as being very reasonable," Vivi responded.

"I'd say the same of Richard so... I guess it depends..."

Vivi nodded. Her phone rang as they drove away then she saw a black limousine pulling up at the front of her building. She knew it was no coincidence.

She didn't want Emmy to know who was on the other end so she answered, "Elvira speaking."

"Elvira, I'm parked outside your building. I thought you might need a ride to work," Richard said.

"Thanks, but I already got a ride."

She wasn't taking a ride from the boyfriend, was she? That thought enraged him.

"Who are you riding with, Elvira?" He spoke the words softly but it was impossible to disguise the anger simmering beneath his words.

"I don't have to answer that question."

Vivi hung up, fueling his anger even more. He would need to know who this other guy was and everything about him.

For now, he was grateful for technology. Richard was able to track her location using her cellphone. Then he pulled down the window in his limo and directed his driver using his GPS tracker.

"Who was that? You went from formal to informal," Emmy commented. Emmy had not noticed the limo as she had focused on the driving.

"It's just a friend who wanted to give me a ride."

"The same *friend* who took you home yesterday?"

"Maybe."

Emmy had never seen Vivi this evasive before and she was intrigued.

Vivi's phone rang again and she recognized Richard's number. She wanted to send it to her voicemail but she didn't want to make Emmy even more suspicious about her mystery caller.

She picked up the phone, "I told you I had a ride."

"But you did not say with whom so be warned that I am now following his car."

His car? She realized he had taken the bait. She turned around and realized the limo was directly behind Emmy's car. He had to be kidding.

Having him follow Emmy's car was not her intention when she answered him vaguely but igniting jealousy was. He had simply complicated her explanations to Emmy.

She replied, "Emmy, a workmate, is giving me a ride."

Richard relaxed. He'd met Emmy when he'd visited the finance department— Terry's Emmy— and he'd liked her.

"That's all I needed to know. Enjoy your ride."

Having assured himself that she was not carpooling with a guy, he instructed Martin to take him to work.

Vivi muttered something inaudible as the limo went by. She was aware of him looking into the car to verify her response as the limo slowed down fleetingly before overtaking them.

Emmy had been driving but had seen Vivi turn around when her phone rang. Then as the limo had cruised by, she knew she had not imagined it slowing down next to her car.

She chuckled, "Could that *friend* be the one in the limo?"

Vivi rolled her eyes, and Emmy took that as a "yes."

"Okay, that is certainly not annoying. I think that was thoughtful of him."

"I think that is being inconsiderate when he went on to follow us even though I told him I had a ride."

"Next time, avoid making him assume you were getting a ride from a guy."

"You're too smart for your own good."

Emmy smiled. She had heard only one side of the conversation between the two but it didn't take much to know what was going on. She also knew who was in the limo but she would not pry for now until Vivi was ready to tell her.

"Thanks, by the way for choosing my humble ride over a grand limo."

"Okay, Emmy. Stop pretending you don't know who that was."

"Well..., let me guess–the boss?" she grinned girlishly.

"Yes, but this will not work for me."

"Why not? Is it because of his status and by that I mean loaded and influential or because you work for him?

"Probably, all of the above. But mostly because he is a nicely wrapped package of trouble."

"You can't possibly know what's in a package until you unwrap. You're the best lawyer I've ever known and you proved that right out of college. You've handled tougher cases."

"But that is different."

"Not really. Even if you think so, I'd have to say Richard is a cool guy. He doesn't strike me as a deadbeat jerk. Don't let your past dictate your present with Richard or your future with any other man. Whoever the guy was, he didn't deserve you. At least give

Richard a chance and let him prove you wrong."

Emmy was the only other person Vivi had confided in about her past. She knew she could count on Emmy to keep this conversation private as well.

Emmy continued, "I have confidence that you can handle *that* package."

Vivi remained quiet, making no comment. Was Emmy right? Could she dare to take a chance with him?

"Look, we're here," Emmy told her minutes later.

Richard arrived at the office excited as he'd been since he found out that Elvira was a floor away from him. As the hours went by he was tempted to stop by her office but he needed a reasonable excuse. After their conversation on the phone that morning, he made sure to call and pay the extra fee required for urgent repairs.

Later that day one of his men returned Vivi's car keys and informed her that her car was in the parking lot. She walked into Richard's office shortly afterwards.

When Marilyn saw Vivi she looked at Richard's schedule. She saw no scheduled appointments with the younger woman.

"He's on a conference call, Ms. Whitman. I can schedule an appointment for later this afternoon?"

Vivi knew some of these so-called conference calls could mean the boss wanted to be alone. She thought to take a chance and see if he was really on a conference call.

"It's important that I speak with him, Ms. Skinner," she said to his secretary.

Marilyn considered the request for a minute. Surely, the boss exuberant mood today is because of this woman? She thought. Hadn't he asked her to clear this schedule when Vivi called? Well, Vivi was here now and calling in person.

She got up and knocked gently then poked her head through the door, "Mr. Mcgallan, you have a guest."

Richard muted his line, aware that Marilyn would never interrupt a conference call unless it was absolutely necessary.

"Who is it?" he asked.

"Ms. Whitman, sir," his secretary replied.

"Send her in, please. I'll see her now."

Richard disconnected the call—glad Terry was on it also. "I have an emergency that needs my attention," he excused himself before hanging up.

It was one of those times he appreciated being the "powerhouse" of a billion-dollar company. He seldom took advantage of the perks that came with it. But the woman who was causing him sleepless nights was in his office. He would not make her wait until his conference call was over. In fact, she was the one he had been looking forward to seeing.

Vivi walked in, looking even more beautiful than when he saw her yesterday. The tinted glass of the limo had not done her justice this morning.

He stood up and walked around his desk. "Is everything okay?" he asked when he was standing before her.

She said to him, "Thanks for my car, Mr. Mcgallan, but here's a refund for my car's expenses."

She had seen clues in her car indicating the garage where her car was taken. Getting the cost of the repairs was easy.

Richard sighed. He should have known she would have objected to him paying for her car expenses.

"No need for refund. You can consider it on the company."

"I need to pay you back, I don't want your money."

"Then have dinner with me and we can consider it paid in full."

"That will not happen."

"Give me a good reason why."

"You are my boss and it will only complicate our work relationship."

"It's only dinner."

"Isn't that how it all starts?"

Richard smiled, "In any case, I'm not accepting a refund from you."

"Then I won't waste my time trying to convince you to take it. I'll give it to Marilyn and let you explain why you can't accept it to her instead."

Then Vivi left his office. As she closed the door behind her, she was unaware of the smile on Richard's face. He chuckled and murmured, "What a spitfire."

The smile faded away as he recalled another spitfire he had met. It felt strange that after many years he still could not get her off his mind so he should be grateful for the distraction Vivi proffered. Picking up his phone he logged back into the conference call.

Later, his secretary came into the office, "Mr. Mcgallan, do you want me to deposit the check written by Ms. Whitman?"

The check was written out to him so she could easily have deposited it without his knowledge. But it was her way of letting him know that Vivi had given her the check.

"That woman could try the patience of anyone and I can't claim to have that virtue," he muttered under his breath.

"Then perhaps you should keep her close and jump on the patience band wagon." Marilynn replied.

Richard was surprised by Marilyn's comment. Up until then, she had simply stood on the sidelines and watched his affairs unfold.

"I beg your pardon?"

"Well, Mr. Mcgallan, with all due respect, a crash course here and there in patience won't hurt you. In fact, I think you can benefit from it. And while you're at it, you might want to stop by the "equal grounds" store and pick up few lessons. I think you might meet Elvira there–on equal grounds. So if you want a chance with her then... just follow along."

Marilyn's perceptiveness and astuteness were indisputable. He trusted her judgement so he nodded, giving her permission to deposit the check.

When she left, Richard pulled out a folder from his desk. He had another meeting with one of his employees–Emeline Weisener.

He'd seen the way his brother looked at Emmy and he could tell this was no mere infatuation. He'd gone into Terry's office one evening and met him gazing out the window. Terry had not responded when he'd called him. Even when he'd walked over and stood next to Terry, his brother's eyes had been transfixed on Emmy who was in the parking lot below his window. Terry was smiling and had a dreamy look on his face like a hungry man staring at a forbidden fruit.

Standing next to him, Richard saw Emmy talking animatedly to one of her co-workers who seemed amused by whatever Emmy was saying. By the time Emmy went to her car, the other woman was laughing hilariously.

It was only when Emmy had driven off did Terry notice him. He'd tried to discourage Terry before but after that, he knew what Terry felt for her was more than he was letting on.

"So why don't you make your move," he'd asked when Terry finally turned towards him.

"I'm not looking for a commitment."

"You are afraid because she is not the type to have an affair with?"

"My point exactly. Besides, she's already taken."

"Not until she says the two words—I do."

"Engagement is basically the same."

Richard looked at him like he was a stranger. "Who are you and where's Terry? You could have fooled me but you're definitely not my brother. Terry would not say that."

Richard tapped him gently on the shoulder. "Hey Terry if you're in there come out."

Terry laughed. "You know I can't do it, Rich."

"What is it you can't do specifically?"

"Neither relationship nor commitment."

"Then you have a serious decision to make, brother. But I cannot help you make it.

He'd decided then to support Terry but stay out of it. So he hoped his upcoming meeting with her would give him insight into Emmy's ability to keep his risk-taking and adventurous brother grounded.

Chapter Six

Ding, Dong.

Off went Emmy's doorbell as Vivi sat waiting for her to complete her makeup. They were going out for dinner but Emmy was not even dressed when Vivi arrived at the apartment thirty minutes earlier. Her Uber ride had shown up sooner than she'd expected. Seeing Vivi, Emmy had rushed to get dressed so she would not keep her friend waiting.

"Could you get the door for me please, Vivi?"

"Yes, but whoever that is will have to wait until you are donc with the makeup before you can talk to him or her. Then we're out of here."

"Okay, thanks."

Vivi walked towards the door not sure if she was able to entertain Emmy's guest until she was ready. She hoped it was Ryan, Emmy's fiancé.

She cracked open the door and felt the rhythmic thudding of her heart as she stared into the metallic dark brown eyes of Richard Mcgallan.

He held her gaze, and as if he had some enchanting powers, she couldn't tear her eyes away from him. What was he doing here? Was Emmy expecting him?

Vivi was unaware of how gorgeous she looked, wearing a pearl pink lace cocktail evening dress. Her silver-like stilettos revealed slender feet with pink polished nails. She was a breath-taking beauty with lips as pink as the dress she was wearing. His eyes never left her lips as she pushed a strand of hair back in place.

Somehow he could sense her surprise so by way of explanation he asked, "Is Emmy in?"

Vivi found her voice, "Of course, come on in."

After all, he was probably here to see Emmy for business purposes. If he wasn't then Emeline Weisener had some explaining to do. Closing the door, she went in search of Emmy but her friend was already on her way out.

"Richard, now that you are here we can leave. I'm famished."

"Then by all means we should get going," Richard replied.

"Wait a minute, I was not aware Mr. Mcgallan was joining us Emmy."

"Richard," he corrected with a raised brow.

"Didn't I tell you?" Emmy asked sheepishly.

Vivi merely stared at her, making no reply.

"Okay, I'm sorry I didn't but could we dine with him please, Vivi? I didn't make reservation on time and he already had a table at the restaurant so he suggested we could join him."

One lift of Vivi's chin and Emmy knew that she was not buying that. "Pretty please, Vivi?"

As Vivi considered Emmy's request, Richard's phone rang.

He spoke into the phone, "Hey Terry."

He listened for a moment then responded, "Could it wait until later? I am about to go to dinner."

Vivi's attention was drawn to the conversation, "Actually, Richard, Terry can join us for dinner—after all, the more the merrier.

Richard knew she wanted to get back at Emmy. But he was glad that Terry could come along.

He extended the invitation to Terry who was only too eager when he learned that Emmy would be there also.

Vivi smiled as she took in the change in Emmy's demeanor. She was not happy about the change in plans. Vivi picked up her purse, glad that she had had the last say.

Dinner went amiably better then Vivi had thought. There was no tension and the conversation flowed easily. Even Emmy and Terry seemed to have called a truce and she realized that they were both amusingly entertaining. So it seemed proper that Emmy would accept Terry's offer to give her a ride when dinner was over, much to Richard's approval.

As they left the restaurant, Richard waited for Vivi to enter the limousine then he went in and sat next to her so that his arm brushed hers slightly. Vivi scooted over slightly.

Richard noticed and asked, "You had a good time?"

"Yes thanks, I really enjoyed the meal. I have no complaints there."

"In my own defense this was Emmy's idea that we dined together."

"I assumed so when you showed up at her doorsteps."

"You know she is trying to play match-maker?"

"Well, the joke is on *her* now."

"Since she ended up getting a ride from Terry?"

"Correct."

She glanced at her watch and he remembered her warning to Terry. *"I'll call her in thirty minutes so make sure to take her directly to her grandfather's."*

"But you're worried about her?"

"Shouldn't I be?"

"Terry would never do anything she doesn't approve."

"Except he is Terry, a renowned philanderer so I have all right to be worried."

"How did you know that Terry is attracted to her?"

"Isn't it very obvious? I'll be surprised if the entire office is not aware of that."

"Both of you seem very close."

Vivi shrugged, "I love her like a sister so I have to protect her from the snarling wolves around here."

"Exactly, the same sentiments she has towards you. Her actual words were, she would allow only a man of honorable intentions to come within five feet of you."

Vivi laughed, "She can be feisty."

He smiled. "Do you think my intentions for you are not honorable?"

"Even if it isn't, I can handle you."

"You can?"

"Of course. Someone reminded me that I have taken on tougher cases."

"I like that. Now let's see how much of me you can handle."

Richard reached over and put his arms around her pulling her close.

She didn't resist because his arms felt warm and reassuring, making her feel protected.

"Does the reason you are resisting me have anything to do with your self-imposed exile?"

She didn't want to ruin their truce so she simply responded, "I don't want to talk about it."

"If you told me, I'd find him and make sure he regrets ever hurting you."

She smiled at the thought of him standing up for her. It made her feel good enough to reply, "I wish I could."

Richard was confused. What did she mean by that? He decided to probe no further instead he let his hands take over the probing.

Richard traveled the next day to begin the process of purchasing another company. Strangely, Vivi realized that she missed him. Was it because of the truce from the night they had dinner or was it because she had anticipated seeing him every day at work?

She kept her phone close by, hoping he would call. As the days went by, anticipation turned into disappointment when he kept silent. But that changed one evening as Vivi snuggled into bed. She'd turned on the bedside lamp and was reaching for the book she had been reading the night before when her phone rang.

"Good evening, beautiful." Richard's deep baritone came on when she answered her phone.

"Look who finally decided to call."

Her voice was light but was that sarcasm he heard? Perhaps he didn't call at the right time.

"Are you available to talk?"

"No, my boyfriend is in bed with me and he doesn't approve of you calling this hour of the night."

"If you intended to make me jealous, then you succeeded. Maybe I should drop everything here and return to Weisener Enterprise."

"What did you expect?"

"Not sure what I expected but definitely not that."

Was she mad at him for not calling or was she mad at herself for her inability to quell the excitement she felt because he was calling?

"So, what made you think about me?"

"You are always on my mind, Elvira. But I also wanted to check in and see if there are any developments in the legal department that I need to know about."

She ignored his first sentence and replied, "You could have called Willie."

"Yes, but I missed hearing your voice."

"If you did, you would not have waited three days to call. But to answer your question, everything is fine on this end."

"Good, and Elvira...my calculations suggest, I have not talked to you for two days, twelve hours, thirty-six minutes, and fifty-six seconds."

He knew the time down to the seconds because he'd had to wait to say goodbye to her before he left. The owner of a company he'd been trying to purchase had issued an ultimatum. They were to purchase his company within a month or he'd accept another offer. She had gone out to lunch with some of the ladies at the office so he'd waited for her. He had glanced at his watch frequently because he didn't want to keep his pilot waiting much longer.

There was silence on her end of the line for few seconds. Was she still there? She was probably surprised by his comment.

"Vivi?" He hadn't called her by her nickname in a long time.

"Yes, I'm here."

She felt the strings pulled at her heart knowing that he'd been counting the time away from her. It made her feel special, like he cared about her more than she'd thought. This was "uncharted waters" for her and it would be best to navigate slowly. "So...how are the negotiations going?

He understood that she needed to change the direction of the conversation. But was the question about work her way of putting him off?

He responded, "Tiring as always. Speaking about that, I should hang up. You need your beauty sleep."

"Good night, Richard."

"Good night, Vivi."

But before he could hang up Vivi spoke, "Richard?"

"Yes?"

"I...want you to know that I appreciate the call."

"It was my pleasure, Elvira."

Days later, Richard sat across from his mom at *Il Ristorante Pasta,* her favorite pasta restaurant. They had been regulars here even before they became a big name in the business world and they still dined at the restaurant. It had the best pasta and spaghetti dishes in the state.

His mother was relaxed now that the fundraising for the foundation was over. It was the week of her birthday and each of her children took turns taking her to lunch.

"So how did the fundraising event go? Did we reach our goal for the evening?"

"It was remarkably successful. We exceeded our goal by an exceptionally good amount so I am extremely glad. It's good to have kids who have the right connections. I appreciate your role in making it a success."

"Glad to be of help, mom."

"Which reminds me, where did you go after the introductory remark? I didn't see you after that," his mother asked.

"I went out to get some fresh air."

Abigail knew better than to pursue the topic. She had her suspicions because she knew her boys but she respected their private lives. Whenever she could, she did give her motherly advice but she'd raised them well so she respected their judgment.

Her attention was drawn to a kid, a few tables across from them, who was slurping his spaghetti with zest. There was sauce all over his mouth while his parents smiled at him adoringly. He looked so much like Richard as a young kid.

In fact, the boy could pass for his kid so she asked, "Richard do you by any chance know the family two tables to your right?"

He looked over at the family his mother had called his attention to, "I don't believe I've met them before. Why do you ask, mom?"

She spread the napkin on her lap and picked up the fork to eat her meal, "Just because that kid looks uncannily like you. I was beginning to think I might have a grandchild whom I've never met."

His mother had been reminding them more frequently that she was looking forward to becoming a grandma. Could this be another attempt at that?

"Mom, if I had a kid, I promise you I would not keep it a secret from my family. You should know I would not run from my responsibility to my child."

"True but sometimes things happen which we might not even be aware of."

He shook his head in denial. His mother was not implying that he could have been careless, was she?

He responded, "Mom, you raised us well to make the right choices. You should be immensely proud of that.

He paused wondering if she was convinced then he added, "We take family seriously which means I will make it my business to know and be involved if there were any chances I had a child by a woman."

She was proud of how her kids had turned out, "Sorry, I didn't mean to pry, Richard."

"I'll be very glad to bring forth your grandkids when I find the right woman."

Why did he have the feeling that might be soon? Why did his thoughts go to the woman he'd call the night before?

His mom smiled at him but couldn't resist thinking, *"I know son but when will you find the right woman?"*

Abigail Mcgallan excused herself to go to the powder room when she'd eaten her meal. Minutes later, the mother of the kid she'd been asking her son about came into the room also. Was this fate?

She could not resist the urge that overcame her to engage in conversation with the woman. This instinct of hers had made her a good lawyer. Although she'd retired, she still followed her instincts when she felt like she had a lead. She still had the gift of getting people to talk.

She looked over at the lady who was freshening up her makeup, "Hello, I'm Abigail. I saw you at the table with your son. He's adorable."

"Thanks, he is a blessing. I'm Brenda by the way."

She was glad Brenda was talking to her so she continued, "Hi, Brenda. I think he looks very much like his dad, don't you think so?"

Brenda debated whether she should tell her the truth since she would have normally replied, *"I think so."*

Abigail noticed Brenda grew incredibly quiet and smiled. Of course she had only made that comment to know if indeed the man was the child's father. The child looked nothing like his father and more like *her* son.

What were the odds that she would see Abigail again, anyway? Brenda thought. The lady seemed to be of an upper class so it was hardly possible that their paths would cross again.

Besides, she felt it was probably time she confided in another person and

Abigail was easy to talk to so she responded, "That is nice of you to say Abigail, but he is adopted."

Abigail understood what that change in her expression was about so she said, "Thanks for sharing that with me, Brenda. He is lucky to have you both as his parents. It's obvious he is well loved."

"Gosh, I love him," Brenda replied.

"Good luck with the teen years," Abigail teased as she left the powder room.

Chapter Seven

Vivi did not go out for lunch because she'd brought lunch from home. Kicking off her shoes, she sat at her desk to eat.

Her phone vibrated and she saw that Richard was calling her on facetime. Excitement bubbled deep within her as she reached for her phone.

"Calling to inquire on the legal department?"

There was no need for cover-up this time, "No, I'm calling to talk to you."

"Shouldn't you be negotiating your latest take-over?"

He chuckled, "Who says I'm not doing that right now?"

Did he just imply that she was his next take-over? "You know, I cannot be taken over by anyone."

"Probably not, but you've definitely taken over here."

"What have I taken over?"

"You've taken over my thoughts, so I'm finding it difficult to focus on the negotiations."

Was he playing with her emotions or did he mean that?

"You should be careful with what you say so that I don't get the wrong impression."

"But I do mean it."

When she did not make a comeback he said, "I was wondering...could you come over to LA? I would like to have an extra pair of eyes look over the papers here."

She was nearly done with the documents she was working on. But she wasn't quite sure if she should just up and leave because he'd asked her to.

"I'm not sure if that will be possible because there is a document that needs my attention."

"Couldn't you pass it on to Willie? I could speak to him about that if you want me to.

She did not want Willie to think that she was getting special favors from the CEO. She could talk to him about working on it until she got back since they sometimes helped each other out.

"I need you here, Elvira, please," he added hoarsely."

Her heart somersaulted beneath her breast. She would go to be the extra pair of eyes, she told herself, not just because she wanted to see him—even though being with him would be her only reason for going to LA.

"I will talk with my colleague and see if he can cover for me until I get back. That means I cannot be in LA for longer than necessary."

Richard took that as a yes. "I will send the company jet for you so be ready tonight at seven o'clock. The limousine will pick you up and take you to the airport."

"Or I could get the evening flight to LA which would cost a lot less money."

"No, you will come with the jet. Seeing you will be worth every penny I spent and even more. Besides, you should know by now that I don't worry about costs."

She was silent for a while, thinking *no you don't need to worry about that, which is why I shouldn't be talking to you right now.*

But even as doubt clouded her mind, she replied, "That depends on whether Willie has no objections to covering for me."

She wasn't going to agree to the arrangements without consulting Willie.

"I'll send you a text if it is okay with him," she told Richard.

"Good, I'll let you go so you can arrange that."

Vivi stared in awe as she took in the interior of the private jet of Mcgallan Incorporated. So this is how the other side lives. It would earn a five-star rating without question.

"Welcome aboard the Mcgallan Bird, Ms. Whitman. We hope you have a nice ride with us," the flight attendant said to her.

"Thank you," she smiled politely.

"My name is Thomas and I will be your flight attendant, please feel free to let me know if I can assist in any way to make your trip comfortable."

She nodded but knew she needed nothing more to make her comfortable in this high-class jet.

Talk about a luxury penthouse on wings with a plush beige colored interior. The cushions in the seat were dark brown accented by leather trimmings. There were four seats arranged around an oak stained table but there were also built in couches with decorative pillows on both sides of the jet long enough to seat a total of eight people.

A bottle of wine on ice and a flute glass sat in the middle of the table. She walked past that to a cabin door which enclosed a private master bedroom complete with an en-suite.

Vivi returned from the room and sat on one of the sofas, closing her eyes. The sound of a phone ringing brought her attention to a table hidden by a sofa chair.

She reached over and picked it up as his voice reached her ears, "Elvira?"

"Good evening, Richard," she responded calmly, glad that he'd call to speak with her.

"I understand the jet will take off shortly, so I wanted to make sure you're comfortable."

"I am, thanks for asking."

Why did he sense withdrawal in her voice? Certainly, she didn't need to be that polite with him? Unless she perhaps was having second thoughts about coming over? He hoped not because he was looking forward to seeing her. He had not been so eager to see a lady for as far back as he could remember. Could this mean something?

"Come safely to me Elvira, I can't wait to see you again," he said huskily.

If he was flirting with her then he was surely skilled at it. She felt it was the sweetest thing he could have said to her at the moment so she murmured, "Me too."

"And one more thing, Elvira..."

"Yes?"

"If your hair is up, let it loose for me, will you?"

He hung up before she could respond. She couldn't let him think she would give in to all his requests. She had let her hair loose but after what he'd said she found her bag and put her hair in a ponytail.

Vivi looked out the window as the jet landed and realized this was not an ordinary airport because, for one thing, the houses appeared closer than they normally would be. The plane taxied to a stop in the backyard of a house. It was nighttime when they arrived but there was no doubt that the house was something akin to a mansion.

It would be an understatement to say it was a great flight. She was given state of the art royal treatment during the flight. The meal was as delicious as any dinner a renowned chef would prepare. She had only had time to grab a quick sandwich on her way home to get ready for the trip so she was glad for the dinner offered.

She thanked the crew and chatted politely with them as she exited the plane. They had been so kind to her, and she wanted them to know that.

"We look forward to seeing you on board the bird again, Ms. Whitman," the flight attendant told her.

She smiled not sure if she would have that opportunity again. Hopefully if she continued working with the company there might be a slight chance of that, but she wouldn't bet on it.

She could hear voices and footsteps as she went down the stairs but she kept her eyes on the flight of stairs. She had to maintain her cool.

What was taking her so long to exit the jet? Richard wondered. He had waited patiently for hours so he could wait no longer. He stood at the end of the stairs and was about to go up when he saw her exiting the plane.

He stood watching her come down the stairs when all he wanted was to walk up the stairs and kiss her passionately. As he'd expected, her hair was pulled back in a ponytail. Contrary to what he'd told her, he wanted it up because he enjoyed letting it loose. She was wearing a pair of skinny blue jeans with a yellow top and a leather jacket.

When she reached the foot of the stairs, his arms encircled her as he captured her mouth. It didn't matter that they were in full view of the crew or that his staff might be looking on, or that they were surrounded by his team of security.

Vivi wondered, why did she feel like she'd come home? Like she never wanted to be away from him again? Like she could entrust him with her heart and know that it will be safe?

She snuggled closer and felt the charm on her necklace rub against her breast. It always reminded her that she had let someone else down. That she had given up the most precious gift she'd ever had. Yet, it was the most courageous and selfless act she'd ever done.

She let him go and pulled out of his arms as guilt overwhelmed her. She'd carried that charm around her neck for the past years. It was proof that she had a past which she could never let go. Would Richard embrace that past if she told him?

There it was again, the withdrawal he seemed to notice. What was it this time? Was it because she remembered that they were still on the airstrip?

"You're right, we need privacy."

He held her hand as he led her through the gates into his mansion.

"How was your trip? Was the service provided by the crew to your liking?"

"They went out of their way to ensure that I was comfortable. And by that I mean bordering on over-indulgence."

He laughed, "That was the instruction they were given."

They had reached the door and he stood facing her. He tucked back a strand of her hair blown by the wind then he pushed open the door to what she thought was a modern-day version of a castle.

Polished marble floors welcomed them revealing a dramatic s-shaped staircase. She was surprised to see members of his staff lined up at the bottom of the stairs. Even more surprised was Richard when he saw Helena, Matthew's kid, walk towards Vivi.

The kid walked over to her and presented her with a bouquet of flowers, "Welcome to Palmridge Haven, Ms. Whitman."

She could hardly contain her surprise as she hugged the kid. Her voice choked on the words, "Thank you so much. This is really kind of you."

She turned to look at Richard but he'd effectively concealed his surprise. He knew without question it was the work of Matthew, who was in charge of operations in the household. Matthew had been advising him lately of the importance of filling the house with kids to "liven" up the home. He made a mental note to thank Matthew because he welcomed whatever made Vivi feel special.

He introduced each of the staff and observed as she acknowledged them, making polite conversation when possible. She did not seem intimidated by what she saw around her. In fact, she looked amazingly comfortable in his world.

"I will take Ms. Whitman to her room now. I'm sure she would like to freshen up for supper."

Vivi was not sure she could have any more food but she did need to freshen up so she did not argue when he steered her towards the stairway.

She didn't know what to make of the welcome she'd just received. Was it customary for all his female guests? The thought annoyed her. Was she jealous? No, she told herself, she just didn't want to fall in the same category as his many girlfriends.

"Not to sound ungrateful and all but you didn't give your staff the wrong impression, did you? I'm here on a work trip," she whispered realizing she was actually trying to convince herself not him.

"I didn't. Matthew runs the house, I just own it. They were probably excited to meet you because it's totally out of character of me to bring non-family members here."

She stopped midway on the stairs to stare at him, "Meaning?"

"Meaning, Elvira Whitman, you are one very special woman."

She had no comeback so she just stared at him in the awkward silence that followed. Then she walked quietly the rest of the way up the stairs.

The extent of his wealth was clearly obvious in the unique elegance of his home. She was thrilled that he had not had private rendezvous with other women here.

"Here is your room, Elvira," he said opening the door to a gold themed room. "Let me know if you would prefer another view of the yard."

"It's beautiful, thank you," she replied, realizing the room had a spectacular view of the garden arrayed in different colors of flowers. Looking around the room, she noticed that her clothes were unpacked and already in the closet.

He pulled her into his arms and kissed her again, reaching up to remove the hairband holding up her hair. Then his fingers combed through her soft black hair. It was pure pleasure he couldn't get enough of.

He'd never felt a woman's hair so soft since...since he was few years younger. He stopped, and Vivi put some distance between them.

Why was the ghost of his past still hunting him? Was it because Elvira reminded him so much of her? He wasn't attracted to her for that reason, was he? He knew his feelings were definitely not influenced by that. He reminded himself that Spitfire was in his past and Elvira was part of his present and maybe future?

"I will leave you alone now."

She nodded but as he turned to leave she asked, "Why, Richard?"

He turned to her, "Why what?"

"Why have you not entertained other women here?"

He walked back to her and rubbed both her arms in an up and down motion, "Because I wanted to bring the right person here, not just any woman."

He hugged her gently then he pulled back to smile at her, "Why? Do you object to my decision to make you the only woman I've brought here?"

Hazel brown eyes twinkled at him then she responded, "No, you made the right choice. You're a smart man. You chose a woman who would not drag you to the altar first thing in the morning after seeing all of this," she waved her hand gesturing to the room.

He threw back his head and laughed, "I'm privileged that you accepted my invitation to come here so it's win-win for both of us."

Chapter Eight

Vivi awakened to the sound of her phone which alerted her that she had slept through the night. Daylight was streaming through the draperies blending with the magic of the room.

It was Emmy on the phone, "I didn't hear from you last night as you promised so I was checking in with you."

"Sorry, I fell asleep after I took a bath."

She looked at the time, "Emmy, can I call you back? I don't want to keep Richard waiting considering that I didn't show up for supper."

"Fine but call me as soon as you get the chance or text me if you can't talk."

As she hung up there was a tab on her door, "Vivi, is everything okay?"

"Yes, I will be out shortly."

Richard went back to his room. He wanted to walk down with her so he'd been patiently waiting.

Minutes later when Vivi emerged out of her room, he was waiting for her in the hallway. He appeared to be in no rush as he kissed her softly.

"How long have you been waiting?"

"Since I woke up this morning," he drawled, his eyes roaming over her and liking what he saw.

The blush rising on her face suggested his point was well taken. "I thought you might need an escort to brunch."

"Thanks. Sorry I kept you waiting again. I hope you did not think I stood you up last night."

"How could I think that since you were sleeping under my roof? Tell me, did you have a good night rest?"

He reached for her hand as they went down the stairs. Would she reject holding hands? Somehow he needed the physical contact.

She let him hold her hand, "Would I sound cheesy if I said I slept like a baby?"

"No, since you *were* sleeping like a baby when I checked on you last night."

She realized that she had not been dreaming when she'd felt his feathery kiss on her jaw. Then he'd tucked the covers securely around her.

She steered the conversation away by asking, "Do you have those papers so I can look over them?"

"Later. Right now, we will eat then we can get to that."

They spend the afternoon in his office, going over the offer drawn up by his lawyers.

Now, they were headed to dinner. He was driving but he still had an entourage of cars behind him.

"So where are we headed for dinner?"

"We're going few miles outside the city."

"How long have you had to travel with a convoy?"

"For probably about seven or eight years."

"Do you sometimes long to get away without them for few hours?"

"Sometimes but they don't like that."

"So does every member of your family have security detail?"

"Yes, although we all have varying number of bodyguards."

He had never really had to worry about the safety of the women he dated because they usually had security of their own but she was different. What would she think if he assigned a bodyguard to her? He couldn't risk her safety even if she would not approve of him getting her one. He may have to assign one of his trusted men without her knowledge. But what if she found out? She would feel like he'd betrayed her, wouldn't she? He would have to take that into consideration as he thought about the inevitable.

Vivi noticed they were now driving in a residential area. There were no restaurants in sight anywhere around. It was also a gated neighborhood.

At the gate he provided the code and name of the resident he was visiting. So we are not going to a restaurant, Vivi thought.

"Are we having dinner with your parents?"

"I hope you don't mind."

"I hope you had informed me before we left your house. Are they expecting us? I'm not sure if I'm ready to meet them."

"They are expecting us and they are looking forward to meeting you."

She pulled down the mirror in the car to check her makeup and to straighten out her hair. She looked down and tried to arrange her top.

Richard parked before one of the homes then his hand covered hers where it was on her chest, "You are beautiful Elvira, and you look elegant. Stop fussing.

He leaned over and kissed her passionately. She'd let her hair down just like he preferred it.

Coming around to the car, he helped her out gently squeezing her hand. He stopped as they neared the door to the house and his hand went around her shoulders.

"Elvira, try to avoid arguing with mom if she misconstrues our relationship to be something more than it is, okay. She is a lawyer also and like you, she thrives on presenting a winning argument."

"But they know that I work for you, don't they?

"Yes, they do," he responded as the door open to reveal the Mcgallan matriarch.

"I'm so glad you could make it, Richie," his mother said hugging him.

"You know I'll always make time to have some of your home cooked meal, mom."

"And who is this beautiful lady accompanying you," she said as she walked over to Vivi.

Richard was not given time to respond before Vivi was enveloped in a warm embrace.

It had been a while since she'd had a hug from her own mom and it felt strange to be hugged by Abigail. She had Vivi longing for her mother's hugs which had made her feel so protected as she was growing up.

She politely extricated herself from the hug and said, "Hello Mrs. Mcgallan."

Richard was not surprised by his mother's warm greeting of Vivi. He had called her to ask if he could bring a friend over for dinner because he really wanted his parents to meet Vivi. He knew from the cars parked outside that his mother had invited the rest of the family. The only car missing was Larry's who might be on his way or probably at work.

"Mom, allow me to introduce Elvira, my ..."

Vivi jumped in smoothly before he could complete his sentence, "his employee. I work in the legal department of Mcgallan Incorporated."

Richard watched as his mother's interest was piqued. She wrapped her hand around Vivi's arm as she walked towards the kitchen, gesturing to Richard to follow along.

"So you must be a lawyer," Abigail stated.

"Yes, I am."

"How long have you been a lawyer?"

"I have been practicing for five years but have only been with corporate offices for the past three years."

"And she is considered among the best if not the best in the business, mom."

That was from Terry who despite the compliment or rather comment he'd just made was staring at her with a guarded expression.

"Of course, you must have met Elvira, Terry. So no introductions are necessary with you."

She turned to her husband and her daughter "Al, Meggie, this is Elvira, Richard's ... employee? She ended looking back and forth between the two.

"Who happens to also be a friend," Richard injected.

"Now, that would make more sense Rich because you've never brought over a female employee or a female for that matter."

"Hello, Elvira," Megan said, hugging Vivi.

"I'm really glad to meet you, Elvira. You came at the right time," Albert Mcgallan said, shaking her outstretched hand.

It's nice meeting you all," Vivi responded.

Albert saw Richard pick a grape from the fruit basket on the table and popped it into his mouth. Then his son leaned against the counter with arms folded. It seemed he was leaving Elvira to stand up to his mom who was sure to pursue the "friend, employee argument."

So Albert continued, "We are in the middle of preparing the meal. What better way to spend time as a family than preparing a meal together?"

His mother asked, "Rich, why don't you help Elvira get an apron?"

He walked to where Vivi stood and reached for her hand, "Come on Vivi, let's get aprons and help out here."

Vivi went with Richard, thinking for a wealthy family, they were seemingly normal. She wasn't sure what she'd expected since she wasn't even aware she'd be meeting them in this setting.

As they passed by his mother she smiled, looking down at their entwined hands, "Uh...huh, Vivi, I'll go with the friend description so you can call me Abigail.

Vivi was glad to get away from the Mcgallan clan for a while even if it was only few feet away.

She stared down at Richard but he only shrugged, "I told you don't try to argue with her. It would have been a lot simpler if you had listened to my advice but you just can't resist the lawyer in you."

He lifted her hair to adjust the apron. His breath fanned her neck as he turned her around to fasten it. His hand gently brushed and lingered on her back as he tied the apron around her. He did not let go when he was done but stood still momentarily, *"If only his family was not on the other side of the room,"* he thought.

"Abby, is it okay if I took our sons away since we are done with the tasks we were assigned?" his dad asked.

"Yes, you may go. We can finish up here and have more ladies time with Vivi."

Vivi and Richard had just completed the tossed salad. He wasn't worried about leaving her alone with his mom and sister who already seemed to be getting along well with her. He looked over at her as he followed his dad and mouthed, "Text if you need me."

"Elvira, would you have reservations about me calling you Vivi?" Megan asked when the men were out of sight.

"Please call me Vivi—that's how my friends call me."

"So, did you meet Richard when he became your CEO?" his mother asked.

"Actually, we met at your recent charity ball."

His mom smiled shrewdly, "No wonder Richard insists you are friends."

"I guess we are friends."

"Mom, are we still going to make the pineapple upside down cake?" Megan asked, thinking her mom may have forgotten about that.

"I think we have enough desserts. Richard won't mind missing out on that for today."

"Missing out on what?" Vivi, asked.

"Pineapple upside down cake is Richard's favorite dessert," Megan explained.

"If you have the ingredients, I could make it quickly," Vivi replied, unable to resist the urge to bake the cake for him.

The two other women looked at each other knowingly and laughed.

"What?" She smiled. "I don't want him to be disappointed when I can whip up a pan of cake easily. Besides you both have your hands full and I am just standing here."

"Right...," Megan teased, sliding a tray of the cookies in the oven and beckoning Vivi to follow her.

Soon they had the ingredients she needed for the pineapple upside down cake and she began to prepare it.

His mom noted her resolve to make the cake and said, "Welcome to our family, Vivi. I don't recall welcoming you formally."

Vivi opened her mouth to object but decided against it and simply replied, "Thank you."

Chapter Nine

Terry Mcgallan wasted no time confronting his brother when they were in the privacy of their father's office, "What is she doing here, Rich? You know she has incredibly low opinion about men of our status."

"Let *me* worry about Vivi, Terry. She is here as my guest."

Terry stared at his brother, "Listen, I know you probably don't want my advice on this but test the waters before you dive in, okay? I don't want to see you get hurt."

Richard walked over to the bottle of wine his dad had retrieved, from the stock in his secret storage behind a rotating bookshelf. He poured some into his glass, "Don't you think I'd know if she had something up her sleeves?"

"Okay..., I'd say we make the most of our time here by watching some sports and you can brief me on the recent merger," their dad told them.

He turned on the television to a tennis match. Both of his sons loved the game and had even competed at the college level.

Just as the players rallied for game point, Abigail announced dinner was ready.

With a click of a button, Albert turned off the television.

"Dad," Terry called out to him, obviously unhappy.

"Your mother called and we have to go, sons. You know I always do as she says."

He heard the chuckled of his sons and said, "I'll tell you my boys, it is the secret to a happy marriage."

Richard thought about those words as they reached the dining room. He looked over at Vivi and his heart swelled with happiness.

Was it the kind of happiness his dad was referring to? Why was he even associating that remark with her when his father had been referring to what makes a happy marriage?

Vivi was aware that Terry continued staring at her with wary suspicion as if she were a poisoned apple his brother had just seen. If it were in a court room, she'd bet he was about to unleash a shocker that would tip the case in his favor. She ignored him, choosing to enjoy the delicious meal and hospitality of her hosts.

"So Rich, mom tells me that she saw a kid who could pass for yours?" Terry asked.

"We are all aware that mom is quite ready to be a grandma."

"But she said the kid was adopted so you might not want to rule out the possibility. You know mom is usually right when she has a hunch."

"Yes, following up on my hunches were critical in helping me during my career as a lawyer," his mother added.

"Adoption could complicate any intent to file for custody should an absent parent even try, don't you think?"

Richard took a sip of his wine, "If I had a kid who was given up for adoption, I'd use every resource possible to gain custody."

"Not if the defense enlisted the expertise of a renowned lawyer like Elvira."

He studied Vivi's reaction then continued, "You still work pro bono on such cases, do you not, Elvira? And I understand you've never lost a case to date in your career?"

Vivi had silently listened to the conversation knowing that Terry had been building a case for this question. She didn't want to get involved in the conversation because it was close to home.

What was Terry getting at? Was he trying to warn her off his brother with instigations that Richard might have a child out there? It should not matter to her since she was not really having an affair with his brother but it did. What if Terry was right? What if Richard had a child with another...? She stopped; she didn't want to entertain such thoughts. Terry knew how to play his cards but she would not buckle down.

She smiled politely, "You are right Terry, I have never lost a case but each situation is different. And I will continue to work pro bono as long as it is not conflict of interest."

Her phone rang and she reached for it, silencing the ringtone.

Richard was sitting next to her and saw Emmy's picture on the screen.

He wanted to change the conversation that his brother was intent on continuing and what better way than to talk about the woman giving him sleepless nights?

"Was it Emeline?" He asked Vivi.

"Yes, I will call her back."

Vivi looked over at Terry and saw the change that came over him, softening his once hostile expression. She knew she had to take a jab at him to turn the focus on him.

"Emmy tells me that you will be sending her over here to learn to use the new software, Terry?"

"I do not wish to discuss the financial department matters with you."

"Just so you know, she'll probably master that skill in no time and be ready to return to her fiancé by the next day."

Emmy was extraordinarily brilliant and the most fun-loving person Vivi had ever known. She was concerned that Terry had an ulterior motive for wanting to bring her to LA.

His jaw twitched at the mention of Emmy's fiancé. It annoyed him that Vivi would bring up Ryan. He had not met him but he was no fan of Ryan.

"Who is Emmy?" Albert Mcgallan asked.

"Why don't we have Terry answer that question, dad," Richard challenged his brother.

"She is the granddaughter of Mr. Weisener," Terry replied, trying to sound detached.

"I've seen a photo of her. She is absolutely gorgeous," Abigail Mcgallan added.

"Who's ready for dessert?" Megan asked coming to the rescue of her brother.

She rose to get the dessert from the kitchen.

"I'll come with you," Vivi followed her glad that she'd gotten her point across to Terry.

Richard took a slice of pineapple upside down cake, "Mmm..., this is absolutely delicious. It seems like you added something to it. What is the new ingredient, mom?"

"That is a secret," his mother answered smiling.

She looked at Meggie and Vivi who were apparently amused at her response. Although Vivi was trying her utmost best to keep a straight face, she chuckled.

"Whatever it is, it's *good*," Richard replied.

"Do you prefer it to the previous recipe I have been using?" his mother asked him.

His father spoke before he could respond, "Don't answer that question, son. Knowing your mom, I suspect it is a trick question."

"I respect dad's judgment on this so I'll have to plead the fifth, mom."

Meggie laughed, "You'd better because that cake was prepared especially for you by Vivi."

"It's for everyone, Vivi offered. "It's the least I could do to contribute to such a gourmet meal."

"Well, since you didn't want to see *him* disappointed, I think you made it especially for him," Megan countered.

Richard was looking at Vivi with such tenderness that she felt her heart skip around in a delightful dance. He reached over and covered her hand on the table.

"Thank you," he whispered.

She nodded, unable to get her words out as his eyes caressed her in a way that only she could notice. Tearing her eyes away from him, she reached for her glass and sipped some wine.

He watched her drink it, reminding himself that they were at the dinner table with his parents. He wanted to feed her a piece of the cake but not with his parents looking on. So he ate the cake on his plate instead.

Richard had informed the staff that they should not wait up for them but his butler had waited around until they arrived.

As they neared the s-shaped stairway Richard said to Vivi, "You look fatigued. Would you like to take the elevators instead?"

Hoping to spend more time in his company, she opted for the stairs, "No the stairs are good."

When they reached the stairs, he lifted her in his arms and carried her until he reached her room.

Vivi did not object. She leaned her head against his chest and just enjoyed the moment.

At the door to her suite, he let her slide to her feet then his mouth captured hers in a kiss that was mind-blowing and breathtaking. Their lips engaged in a private conversation as their hands twirl in on the excitement.

How did he get her to let down her defenses of many years? Here she was in his world yet she did not feel like a stranger in it. What would he think if he found out about the secret that had haunted her for years?

Richard wanted to do more than stand before her door and kiss her. He felt her heart thudding or was it his own racing to meet hers?

Her moans were soft and inciting. She shivered as his firm and muscled torso sent warmth seething through her. She warmed up at his every touch.

His hand roamed over her and he pleaded hoarsely, "Invite me in Vivi, please?"

She became still, "I'm not ready for...you know..."

"Would you invite me in if I promise to wait until you are ready?"

Vivi did not understand. Hazel brown eyes stared at him, "If you will wait until I am ready then... why would you still want to come in?"

One large hand cupped her face. He wasn't sure how they could spend the night either but he didn't want to let her go. Not yet, so he replied, "Because I just want to hold you tonight."

She wanted that as much as he did, "Then you can be my guest for the night, Richard.

"It would be a dream come true," he replied and holding her hand they stepped into her room.

Vivi stirred and snuggled closer inflaming Richard's desire for her. His eyes flew open and he lay awake to her warm body spooned against him and her head cradled on his arm.

They were both fully dressed in the clothes they wore to dinner. He would not risk giving her a chance to change her mind so he'd just pulled her to the bed and into the crook of his arm. They had talked long into the night until she fell asleep, and then he'd fallen asleep also.

Now the glow of the morning sunlight filtering through the window panels reminded him that it was far past the time he usually woke up. His wristwatch confirmed it was two hours past his wake-up time.

He had made it through the night without doing more than talking. It was a historic first for him but given the choice of sleeping alone or simply lying next to Vivi, he would choose being cuddled with her.

An alarm clock went off and Vivi reached over for her phone then switched her position so that she was lying on her back.

She looked up at him and smiled, "Good morning."

Had he ever seen a radiant smile so alluring or heard a greeting so heartwarming? Why did he feel like this was what he wanted to wake up to for the rest of his life?

He could tell that there was a well-kept secret she had yet to reveal. He hated secrets and was skeptical about women who kept them from him. So why did it not matter when it came to this woman? Didn't he consider secret a game changer in his affairs? It seemed as if he was constantly modifying his rules to keep her in his life. Was it because he was falling for her?

He smiled at her then reached over and planted a soft kiss on her lips as his hand reached up to cover one of her breasts, "Good morning, babe."

She shivered at the endearment and put some distance between them, "I have to get ready."

He raised a brow wondering why the hurry to get ready. As far as he was concerned on a Sunday there should be no rush to get out of bed.

"How far away is the nearest church?"

Okay, that was the reason for the rush. "It's only about five minutes away."

"Can Martin give me a ride there?"

"Certainly," he replied getting off the bed to give her privacy.

He walked to the door, turned to her and said, "Thanks for a great night, Elvira. It was amazing."

That compliment put a smile on her lips and she hummed as she did her morning care.

Chapter Ten

Vivi sat next to Richard in a comfortable sofa as they went over the legal papers for the new acquisition. He briefed her on his ideas for the new company and she listened attentively.

Later, he excused himself to call his grandparents, "They called me when we were in the church and I make it a priority to call them as soon as I get the chance."

He continued to show her his caring personality in little but sincere ways. He had even surprised her by accompanying her to the church.

When he had shown up at her suite to walk her to breakfast, he was dressed in a light blue designer long sleeves shirt and a tie with matching dark blue pants.

She'd hoped he was going with her to church but wasn't quite sure until he took her hand and led her to the waiting car in his driveway. She had requested something simpler than a limousine so he had asked Martin to bring around his Maybach Mercedes Benz.

Now, she was touched that he prioritized talking to his grandparents over work, "Please go ahead and call them."

At the sound of his voice, his grandmother remarked, "Carl, look who finally decided to call back."

"Sorry, about that granny, I was in church when you called."

"Church? You went to church? Carl, you need to hear this, Richard went to church today."

He saw his grandfather come running over. He had made sure all his grandparents were set up on skype. By seeing them on skype, he could assure himself that they were fine. They relished their quiet life out of the limelight but he provided maximum security regardless.

His grandfather said, "Well let's see, it is not Easter or Christmas and you are not visiting me so..."

"I took a friend to church."

"You mean you took Elvira to church?"

He chuckled, "Do you know about Elvira?"

"Everyone knows about Elvira. She is having a positive influence on you too, I can see that" his grandmother said.

"Where is she anyway? Could we talk to her?"

"She is busy right now but I'll see if she can spare a moment."

Elvira had been focused on the documents before her, trying to block out the conversation going on few feet away from her. But when she saw Richard beckoning her to come over, she put the papers away and stood up.

She did not want his grandparents to think she and Richard were having an affair but there was no harm in greeting them. So she stood up and walked over to where he sat skyping with them.

"Elvira, meet my grandma and grandpa Mcgallan."

"It is very nice to meet you, Mr. and Mrs. Mcgallan."

"You can call us gramps and granny, my dear," his grandmother said.

She turned towards Richard inquiringly, "I don't know if..?"

Richard cut off the question he sensed she was trying to ask, "Why not?"

133

"You know Betty, I think we are going to get along with her very well," his grandfather said.

"Yes, she seems smart and polite," replied his grandma.

"She is all that and a sight for sore eyes too. I'd say we are on the way to being great grandparents, don't you think Betty?"

It was time to correct all the assumptions. She looked at Richard but he seemed to challenge her to argue about his grandparents' speculations.

"Sorry to disappoint you but Richard and I are just...friends."

"Yes, yes, we heard," both grandparents responded in unison.

At that moment, his phone signaled another incoming call.

"Granny, gramps, we have to go now. Gramps and granny Harris are on the line."

Vivi sat at the conference table in the company's head office and discussed clauses and lines of the proposed contract that needed renegotiations. She presented her arguments regarding the recommended changes and defended them convincingly.

She had spent the day before scrutinizing the papers and researching like she did when she prepared for a case. She barely noticed Richard who sat quietly, observing her make the case for her suggestions.

He was glad he had called Vivi to look at the papers. He trusted his team of lawyers because he hired the best but she brought a fresh perspective to the negotiation table.

He admired her tenacity and appreciated her concern not only for the company but for the wellbeing of the employees. Now he understood why she had been as successful in her career as she was.

Her phone rang shortly and she got up, "I have to take this call. Be right back."

When she walked back into the room he knew something was amiss. She appeared frightened and he saw her hands shake as she lifted up a stack of papers and passed them to the nearest corporate lawyer, "I highlighted some lines that you might want to recheck. I also wrote comments where necessary."

She had earned the respect of the team and her colleague asked, "Why don't you present them? It might have the most effect if the team heard it from you."

"Sorry, I've got to go...family emergency," she said by way of explanation to the group.

She sped out of the room unaware of the stare from the group around the table.

Richard hurried after her instructing his team leader to continue with the meeting and get back to him.

"Hold on, talk to me Elvira. What's going on?"

She was busy on her phone, dialing airline numbers. "Can't talk now, I have to find a flight back to San Francisco."

Did she even realize that he deserved an explanation? Granted he'd asked her to come over mostly because he wanted to see her but it was only polite to explain why she had to leave in such a rush.

"You can take the jet."

He punched numbers and issued instructions.

"You parents need your jet, Richard, I am calling an airline," she responded as she was put on hold by the ticketing representative. His parents had talked about their plan to use the jet when they had dinner with them.

He held her hand and pulled her to the elevators, pushing the button for the lower floor. She was so upset that she just appeared to be forcing air into her lungs. He had to do something to calm her down.

He pulled her into his arms, "Whatever happened, it will be alright."

He closed his eyes and prayed silently that he was right. He didn't want to give her false hopes but he had to try to help her feel better.

"It's my...my friends' son. He was jumping on the bed, fell off and injured his head, badly."

"How bad is it?"

"Surgery bad."

His arms around her tightened but Richard had questions he wanted to ask her. Like what was it she was not telling him? He could sense that she did not tell him the whole story. First she'd said "family emergency" but now she just told him her "friends' son" so which was it?

"You're sure you don't want me to accompany you to the waiting room?"

"Yes, I'm sure but thanks anyway. You've done enough already. Besides, I think Ben and Brenda might not be up to receiving guests.

They were standing before the elevator in the hospital. She'd asked that he should not walk her into the hospital but he had insisted on following her until she was on her way in the elevators. He hugged her as the elevator doors opened to allow her entry then he stood looking as the doors closed taking her to the floor of the surgical unit.

Richard walked back to his car waiting outside the hospital entrance and Martin drove off. He pulled out his phone to make some calls just as his phone buzzed.

"How's she doing?" It was his mom calling to check up on Vivi.

He'd had to reschedule his parents' trip to be able to get Vivi to San Francisco on the jet, "I just dropped her off at the hospital."

"Why didn't you go with her?"

"She didn't want me to, mom. She said something about her friends' needing their privacy."

"And you didn't insist on accompanying her? You should've gone along regardless, Rich."

He realized his mother was right. This was one of the times he should have insisted but he didn't. Should he go back to the hospital?

Dr. Morris walked to the waiting room to meet with the parents of his patient. He had to confer with the parents before proceeding with the next step.

Brian, the patient, had been brought to the ER with an injury to the head after falling off a bed. X-rays and CT scan showed no other major injuries. The doctor was concerned that Brian had lost lot of blood.

"Mr. and Mrs. Elliot?" he asked when he reached the lobby.

Three people stood up and walked towards him. There was a middle-aged couple and a younger woman. He assumed that the couple, who appeared to be clinging to each other for support were the boy's parents. Was the other lady the aunt or perhaps another family member? She seemed equally as distressed as the parents, if not more distressed.

He invited them to a private room, "We have been able to get the bleeding under control but Brian lost lot of blood. He is being prep for surgery but he will need blood transfusion."

He paused before he could ask the next question. Somehow he wondered if any of the people in the room would be able to donate blood to Brian. He knew if any of them could donate blood then his suspicion might be unjustifiable.

"I'm sure you are aware that Brian has a rare blood type?"

"Yes, we learned that when Brian was very little," Mrs. Elliot replied.

The doctor nodded, "His blood type is $RH_{(null)}$ also known as the "golden blood." In our world today, less than one hundred people have that same blood type, so it is very scarce."

He looked pointedly at the father then he said, "Presently, we do not have that blood type available in the blood bank except the ones reserved for the nearest donor. So is there any family who could donate a pint of blood before he goes into to surgery?"

He noticed the couple eyes turned to the other woman in the room.

Mr. Elliot spoke to her, "Vivi?"

She shook her head, "No, I'm afraid not?"

"We adopted Brian when he was a baby, doctor," explained Mrs. Elliot.

Vivi asked, "You said there is some blood reserved in the bank for the nearest donor. Couldn't some of that be used for Brian?"

Dr. Morris rubbed his hand over the charm that rested in his pocket. He had hoped they would reach this point in the discussion.

"I will have to contact the donor for his approval. There are regulations regarding how often a donor can donate blood. He is presently unable to donate because he did so recently but I am sure he won't hesitate to give his approval. He happens to be my cousin."

"Please, help our son, Dr. Morris," Mrs. Elliot said.

"I will make that call to him now."

Dr. Morris excused himself as he pulled out his phone and placed the call. He wasn't considering hospital protocols and procedures because he was willing to take that chance.

Richard listened as his mom explained their plans for the trip she and his dad were taking to Las Vegas. But he thought about her advice that he should not have let Vivi go alone to the hospital. His phone displayed an incoming call at that moment.

"Mom, I've got to take a call coming in. It's Larry on the other line."

"Okay, call me later once you hear from Vivi. I want to know how the kid is doing."

"I'll be sure to do that."

He switched over glad that Larry was calling since he needed Larry's help any way.

"Hi Larry, you're just the person I need to talk to right now."

"That's good to know because I was wondering, how quickly can you get over to San Francisco?"

"I'm already in San Francisco. Why do you ask?"

"How quickly can you stop by at my workplace? There is an urgent favor that I need to ask you but I'll let you know when you get here."

"That's no problem. I'm close by. I'll be there in about five minutes."

Dr. Morris gave him the directions to the waiting area of the surgical unit. Then he hung up and waited for Richard to arrive.

Chapter Eleven

Richard exited the elevators and came face to face with Vivi and a couple. He thought the couple appeared vaguely familiar but he could not remember where he'd seen them.

"I specifically told you it was best if I came here alone, Richard," Vivi told him when he walked over to her.

"Actually, I called him. Richard is my cousin," Dr. Morris said entering the room.

"Your cousin whose blood type is $RH_{(null)}$?" Mrs. Elliot asked.

"Yes."

Hearing the mention of his blood type give him a hint of why Larry had called him to the hospital. They'd always referred to the hospital as Larry's workplace which in fact it was.

"Richard, I have a patient, Brian, who needs a pint of blood. Since you are in the restriction period I was hoping you could authorize release of a pint of blood reserved for you in the blood bank."

Although Richard lived in LA he visited San Francisco, frequently for business so he had some blood reserved at the blood bank there.

"Definitely, let me know what I need to do?" He answered in response to Larry's question.

Then Richard turned to Vivi to confirm what he already assumed, "Is Brian the son of your friends?"

"Yes..., he is," she looked at the couple.

Realizing she needed to make introductions, Vivi said, "Richard I'd like you to meet Brenda and Ben Elliot."

"I'm sorry about your son, Mrs. Elliot," Richard said reaching for the hand of the boy's mother.

"Please, call me Brenda."

"And you can call me Ben," the man responded.

"Larry, I will be very glad to do whatever I can do," Richard told his cousin.

Dr. Morris completed the process of getting the required authorization from Richard. He knew without a doubt that there was definitely something that didn't seem quite right.

He felt the charm in his pocket once again. It was definitely the charm he'd made for Richard years ago. Dr. Morris had become orphaned at a young age and his aunt Abigail had taken him into her home.

One day Richard had come home from school complaining that some kids had called him teacher's pet. They were mad because he'd made sure to tell the teacher when another kid was being bullied.

His teacher had given him a yellow star which he had proudly displayed in his room. Larry, who was four years older than Richard, had carved him a charm in the shape of a star and engraved his initials "RM" on the back of the star.

He had said to him, "You are a star, Rich. Shine bright wherever you go and always remember your star will help you find a way out when you need it."

He looked at Richard who was now attentively engaged in a conversation with Vivi. He'd learned that Richard had taken a friend to their parent's home. What was her connection to the family whose kid he was treating and how long had she known his cousin?

When he had held Brian's hand in a comforting gesture, as he usually did to his patients, he had felt the object in the boy's hand. A nurse later told him that Brian had been clutching the charm when he was brought into the emergency room. Could it be mere coincidence that the child clutching the charm had the same rare blood type as his cousin or was it something of significance in this situation?

Now, Larry decided, was time to hand over the charm to the boy's mom. Hopefully, Richard would take his eyes off Vivi long enough to see the charm.

He reached for the charm, "Mrs. Elliot, you might want to keep this so that Brian doesn't lose it. The nurse said he was holding on to it when he came in."

Richard was conversing with Vivi but raised his head slightly as Mrs. Elliot reached for the charm dangling from a black leather necklace in Larry's hand. He gulped, wondering if he was hallucinating. He walked over in an attempt to get a closer look at the charm—*his* lucky charm. He could recognize it no matter what.

His stomach knotted and he could not seem to release the air filling his lungs. He felt cold sweat break out all over him as he drew closer.

"May I take a look at your son's charm, Mrs. Elliot?" he asked, his voice sounding raspy.

Unsure of his seemingly engrossed interest in it, she passed it on to him, "It is Brian's lucky charm. He carries it everywhere with him."

Richard held his breath as he turned over the charm and saw the initials—his initials— in bold letters on the back of it. He remembered nine years ago when he had last held it in his hand.

How could he ever forget the overwhelming passion he'd shared with one amazing woman? It had been at a masquerade ball and she had insisted that their identity remained incognito so they had not removed their masks. He could never forget the silkiness of her skin when he'd placed the necklace around her neck with the promise, *"This charm will lead me back to you no matter how far apart we might go physically.*"

He was back in that room, hearing her laugh out cheerfully, *"It may but I'd give you a run for your money before it does."*

She was right; he had yet to find her. It couldn't be Brenda Elliot, could it? There was absolutely no attraction between the two of them.

He opened his mouth to ask the question he could not resist asking then he hesitated. He looked over at Vivi who was still standing few feet away, staring absent mindedly at a chair. How would she react to him having a kid and how might this information affect their relationship? He forced his thoughts back to the charm in his hand.

He glanced nervously between the couple and suddenly he realized where he had seen them before—at the restaurant. Their kid had been slurping spaghetti.

"How did...Brian get it?" He asked, his hands now beginning to shake as he waited for her response.

"His birth mother gave it to him on the day we took him home," Ben Elliot responded to his question.

He could not jump to conclusions now. But why would Brian's birth mother give it to him? There were so many pieces to the puzzle that he needed to solve to find out the truth. He knew there were too many connections to be coincidental. He needed to know if he had a kid.

"His... birth... mother? Do you know who she is?"

Brenda jumped in unsure of his sudden interest in Brian's mother, "Yes, we do, why?"

She had made a promise to Brian's biological mother and she would keep it. She was grateful that he was helping Brian but she could show her gratitude in other ways.

Sensing Brenda's reaction Richard went into negotiation mode, "This might sound weird coming from me a stranger whom you've just met but could you tell me the name of his biological mother, please?"

"No, I'm afraid not. We gave her our word that we would never disclose that information," she replied.

Okay, thought Richard. Perhaps some incentive might motivate Brenda to be more cooperative.

"I assure you I am willing to use whatever resources to gain access to that information."

It was a subtle but most times effective line his rivals deemed irresistible. He respected her loyalty but this was a vital piece of information he needed.

Vivi had barely noticed Richard walk over to talk to Brenda. She was overwhelmed with guilt and she willed Brian to fight his way to recovery. She was unaware of the conversation going on around her until Richard's last statement.

She saw Brenda glance her way nervously then responded, "Sorry, but the only resource you have that is of essence to me at this time is a pint of blood for my son."

"I'm interested in reaching out to her because I need to know how she got the charm."

Vivi decided enough of it, she had lived with this guilt for long enough but not after today.

"His biological mother got that charm from his biological father, Richard, stop badgering Brenda."

He turned to Vivi who had come to join them, "How would you know that Elvira?"

She stood up straight, shoulders squared, head held high, and she walked over to where he stood, "Because I'm his birth mother."

There, she'd told him; she would not deny her son when he needed her most. She had given him up to ensure he got the care he needed which she was unable to provide for him at the time but she'd never stopped loving him. She had insisted on an open adoption because she couldn't just let him go.

The two stood facing each other as he processed the information she'd given him. He'd spend years trying to find her alias Spitfire until he met Vivi. Looking at her daring stance, he was unaware of the anxiety and guilt consuming her. Although he was livid with her at the moment, he thought her challenging pose was sexy and his body responded in kind. But he would not be diverted, not now, when he might be the father of the little boy she had given away.

"*Spitfire*?"

Vivi shook her head; he couldn't possibly know that except— "No..., it can't be," she said in denial.

Vivi's heart somersaulted when she saw him nod. His alias couldn't be the *Green Arrow*, could he? How had she been captivated by him not once but twice? Perhaps she should count her lucky stars that she had not gotten head deep in before it was too late this time.

This was one of the many times skills developed as a lawyer give her an advantage. She recovered from the shock of what she'd just discovered.

Richard could not stop the barrage of questions that came rolling out as his mind tried to process the shock.

Vivi, however, did not flinch when he babbled, "How did it happen? I took the necessary precaution to protect you."

He didn't care that the others in the room were staring in disbelief at the real-life soap opera they presented.

She shrugged, "You know what they say, Richard—99.9% accurate. So we were part of the 0.1% that fell off the accurate train."

"So you choose to give him away rather than be bothered? He is our little boy, how could you? I would never have thought you were uncaring but I guess I was wrong. Did that night mean anything to you at all? Was giving him up meant to be a slap in my face?"

"You really think this was about you, Richard? It was never about you. It was the best thing I could do for Brian. At that time, I couldn't give him what Brenda and Ben were able to give him."

He held out the charm, "You had this. You could have found a way to contact me. This is the digital age, Elvira. You're intelligent enough to have known what to do."

"And have you thinking that I wanted your money? I didn't even know your actual name. How sure was I to know that you wouldn't have denied any connections when you learned a child was involved?"

"I'd never have denied my child, Elvira. It was your suggestion that we remained incognito, wasn't it? Now I understand why you insisted. It was to protect your parents and you. That was the same reason why you gave our child up too, wasn't it? You didn't want your father to know that the pastor's daughter wasn't as innocent as he may have assumed?"

Did it hurt to hear his accusations because it came from him or because that was the actual reason for giving up her son? Would she even have thought about giving Brian up for adoption if she had not been ashamed that she'd betrayed her parents' trust? But Richard was equally as responsible as she was so she could not let him make her feel guilty for doing what was right for her child under the circumstances.

"Shut up, Richard," she yelled at him.

It was the first time Richard was spoken to with such insolence so he was taken aback. He was so stunned that he couldn't find his voice. He ignored the persistent ringing of his phone as he stared at her.

Realizing that he had calmed down for a moment Vivi said, "Now is neither the place nor the time to engage in this argument. Right now, Brian needs us.

She turned to the child's adopted parents and his doctor, "He needs the support and love of all of us as he recovers."

She was glad that Brian's doctor was Richard's cousin. It was also comforting that Richard was his biological dad. Just knowing that he was there made her hopeful that Brian would be alright. Hadn't he said so himself even before they were both aware that he was in fact Brian's dad?

Chapter Twelve

Richard listened as his cousin met with them after the procedure on Brian, "It all went well and he is responding well to the transfusion so he should be fine. He might experience headache over the next few days and he will be given some pain killers."

"Can I see him, Larry?"

"Come on, I'll walk with you. He is in recovery."

"We need to see him, Dr. Morris," Mrs. Elliot told him.

"Since he is in recovery I will suggest at most two visitors at a time. So since Richard is coming along, I will suggest one more person."

Brenda turned to Vivi, "You can go Vivi. I'll go with Ben."

"If you don't mind, can I go alone this time? It will be my first time meeting him." Richard told Vivi without looking at her.

Since receiving the information, it would be his first time seeing the son he did not know existed. He wasn't quite sure how he would handle the encounter considering that he was still shaky after learning the fact.

She didn't want to make a fuss of it so Vivi nodded. It wasn't fair of him to ask that but she would let him go alone.

"This way," Dr. Morris directed, glad to finally be alone with his cousin.

"How bad is it, Larry?

"The images we took don't show trauma to the brain so he should be going home in about two days."

He didn't want Richard being alarmed so he continued, "Don't be alarmed by the bandage, it's not as bad as it looks. We need to keep the wound clean so to prevent the bandage from coming off we had to run the bandage around the head. He might still be under sedation."

Richard nodded. They had reached the recovery room. He noticed that there were only four kids in the room but there were medical equipments almost everywhere.

Dr. Morris led him to a bed near a window. Richard's heart thudded as he drew near the bed and he felt the hair rising on his skin.

He stared at the child lying asleep on the bed, head bandaged as Larry had said. The child appeared restful but it was obvious he had been through a lot.

My son, he thought. He wasn't surprised to see that Brian was the little boy he and his mother had seen. He couldn't resist reaching for the child's hand. It was folded into a fist but he covered it with his own. Was he trying to be brave? Is that why his hand was curled into a fist? He sighed when he realized that was what *he* had done as a kid.

"You will be alright, son. Did you know that your doctor is also your uncle?" he choked on his words.

What if anything happened to his son? Would he be able to forgive Elvira? What would he do? He was worried and frightened.

He did not feel the tear rolled down his cheek until he saw the tear drop on his son's cheek. He brushed it away and wiped his face. Then for the second time that day he prayed that Brian would be alright.

"Don't worry, son. When this is over, you will be coming home with me," he whispered.

"Umm..., I think I should bring the Elliots and Elvira in to see him also,"

Dr. Morris suggested, hoping to distract Richard.

As they left the recovery room, the doctor's phone beeped. It was his aunt calling.

"Is Richard okay? Because the last time I spoke with him he was on his way to see you and now he is not taking my call."

"He is here with me Aunt Abigail," Larry told her passing the phone on to Richard.

"I think Aunt Abigail deserves to know that she has a grandson. She needs to hear it from you so don't make me be the one to tell her."

Richard nodded and took the phone, "Mom, you were right all along."

"About what," his mother asked on the other line.

"I have a son, mom. The kid we saw at the restaurant is mine. He's here at the hospital."

It was bitter-sweet news. She was elated to learn that she had a grandchild but worried that he was in the hospital.

"How is he? Is he going to be alright?" she asked anxiously.

"Larry said he should be able to leave here within couple of days."

His mother said to his father, "Al, we have a grandson who is in the hospital."

Then she said to Richard, "We will be flying over right now" and she hung up.

Her husband nodded. They were on their way to the airport but Vegas would have to wait, being with their grandchild was more important.

Vivi sat quietly with the Elliots at one end of the waiting room while Richard stood on the other end, pacing the floor.

He'd barely said two words to her since he came from seeing Brian in the recovery room. It seemed he couldn't even bare to look at her. When he came out from seeing their son, she had gone to him as the Elliots went in to see Brian.

"How is he doing," she had asked.

Once again without looking at her he had answered, "Holding on." Then he had walked away to make a call.

What was he thinking? What was he planning with respect to Brian? She

161

wanted to go over to ask him but he seemed so cold, so withdrawn.

He went to talk with the Elliots when they returned from visiting with the child.

"I want to thank you for what you've done for my son. I am willing to compensate you for everything. But I must let you know that I am filing for custody."

Ben frowned at him and replied, "We don't want your money, Mcgallan. Brian is our son and you will not take him away from us."

"I am his biological father and I will take over custody of him now."

"No, you won't," Vivi spoke up. "How cruel can you be? Are you even thinking about Brian? What do you think it's going to do to him if you snatched him away from Ben and Brenda, the parents who have cared for him these years?"

"Elvira, my son is my responsibility not someone else's."

"We'll see about that. Don't forget I'm also his biological mother and I entrusted him to their care. They have been wonderful parents to him. For all your wealth and influence, you will not take him away from them—not if I can help it," she responded.

"See you in court, then," he responded and went back to pacing at the other end of the room.

The entire Mcgallan clan arrived in style at the hospital, complete with their security detail which added to the size of the group.

"How is he, Richard? Where are his adopted parents?" his mom asked.

"He is still in recovery but Larry said he will be moved to his room soon."

His family had all gathered around him and didn't seem to have noticed the other visitors on the other end of the room.

"His adopted parents are Ben and Brenda Elliot," he said pointing to the couple.

It was then that his family turned to see the couple. His mother was already reaching out to them.

"Vivi, I did not see you when we entered. Brenda and Ben must be your friends, I take it?" she asked as she shook hands with the couple then reached out to give Vivi a warm hug.

His sister also turned and walked over to Vivi, giving her a hug.

"Yes, they are," Vivi replied.

"How are you holding on, son? Albert asked, sensing the tension emanating from his son.

"It hasn't been easy trying to process all the information coming at me at once. But I have to be strong for my son, dad."

His brother Terry who had also come along with the group stared at Vivi. He sensed something was off. Why was she on that end? Shouldn't she be standing next to Richard?

"Do they know who his biological mother is?" he asked.

"Yes, she has been in contact with them. It was an open adoption."

"So where is she in all this, Rich?"

"Right there, standing next to Megan."

"You can't be serious," Terry asked in astonishment as his eyes went to the only other woman standing next to his sister.

"It's her alright."

Terry could not keep the skepticism out of his voice when he asked, "Was she trying to blackmail you? Is that why she has been trying to come around?"

"Judging by her reaction when she realized I was his dad, I'd say she didn't know either. She seemed genuinely surprised to know I was his father."

"Okay, I'm confused. Why would she not know and why were you not told about the kid?"

He briefly explained where he'd met Vivi and what had transpired before his family arrived.

"I'm sure there is a very reasonable explanation for which Vivi gave him up for adoption," his father injected.

"I still have to hear that, dad," Richard responded still convinced that she had selfishly given up their kid for adoption.

"I'll be right back, son," Albert told Richard as he walked over to the family on the other end of the room.

Larry came out to talk to the group and saw the rest of the family. He eagerly greeted them, glad to see them all. He was as professional as he could be, making sure to talk to Brian's adopted parents but also including the rest of the family as he updated them on the child's status.

When Larry finished talking, Albert greeted the Elliot's then he put his arm lightly on Vivi's shoulders and spoke to his wife, "Abby, Vivi needs you."

It was a caring statement which reminded her of the many times she'd heard her father speak those words to her mother. As a child and until she left the security of her parents' home, those words had reminded her that she could always count on her family during difficult times. She felt tears welled up in her eyes. She had been holding on well but she knew she had to get away before she gave in to the emotions overwhelming her.

Abigail took one look at Vivi and said, "Larry, where is a room for privacy?"

"This way," he replied.

Abigail held Vivi's hand as they followed Larry. The doctor had barely closed the door when Vivi began to sob.

Chapter Thirteen

Abigail sat with Vivi soothing her with gentle words as the tears flowed. Vivi's shoulders shook with sobs and she didn't hold back the emotions she'd kept hidden for nearly ten years. Gradually, the sobs became sniffles and she felt like a weight had been lifted off her shoulders.

When she was sobbing, she did not hear Richard come into the room under the pretense of delivering coffee to them. Neither did she see the exchange between both mother and son as Abigail silently mouthed, "Thank you" to her son.

Vivi accepted the tissue Abigail passed onto her. She wiped her eyes and blew her nose then she sighed, "Sorry, I didn't mean to have a complete meltdown."

"Don't worry about it. My shoulders are available to you anytime if you need them to cry on."

Abigail motioned to the cup of coffee closest to Vivi, "You should drink that while it is still hot."

She reached for her own coffee also but watched as Vivi took a sip of the hot liquid. It was obvious that it was to her liking.

Vivi realized someone had to have brought the coffee into the room and seen her in a vulnerable state. She hoped it was Megan because she didn't want Richard to have seen her.

"Richard brought them," Abigail offered, sensing the question she wanted to ask.

Vivi winced, "Did he see me... in tears."

His mother nodded, "Don't take his bark seriously. He is concerned about you even though it may appear as if he isn't. Besides, he is still recovering from the shock of the past hours so I'm sure he understands your reaction.

She groaned, "His anger seems to be directed at me and I don't get it because all the decisions I've made were made to ensure Brian's wellbeing."

"Did it occur to you that he might be angry at himself for not revealing his identity when you first met?"

"He seems to think I give up Brian to protect my parents and me from scorn by acquaintances."

"So is he right for thinking that?"

"No, I kept Brian for three months. I couldn't tell my parents because I'd failed them. I wanted to keep him but it was so financially difficult. I knew it would be selfish of me to keep him. I wanted what was best for him."

"I understand."

"How can you understand when you have never been in that situation before?"

"Oh, I had similar experience when I had my son and we lost his dad."

Vivi raised her heard sharply, "Richard?"

"Yes, Richard is Albert's adopted son."

She knew Vivi was interested so she continued, "Richard was a baby when we lost his dad. It was exceedingly difficult for a while. I met Albert on a bus when I was on my way to an adoption agency. I sat next to Albert and I was crying the entire bus ride. Albert was on his way to work. He was working at a grocery store then. He did not say a word to me on the bus but when I got off the bus he also got off.

He stopped me and asked why I was so sad. Wanting someone to talk to I explained my problem. He said I didn't need to give my baby up. He took us in and we were roommates for about a year before we started dating."

"That was very noble and generous of him."

"Yes, my Albert is a gentleman and our boys had a very good teacher."

"Richard wants to file for custody but I feel we need to think about Brian in all of this. I'm worried about how the decisions we make will affect him?"

"I think Richard needs some time to process this then you can talk to him about doing what's best for Brian. If you try to talk to him now you will only enhance his resolve to file for custody."

Vivi nodded realizing that Richard's mom was right. She would give him time but if he carried out his threat, she would meet him in the court.

Vivi had called Emmy when she arrived at the hospital; shortly before Dr. Morris called Richard. Emmy arrived at the surgical waiting room and was surprised to see the Mcgallan family fully present at the hospital. So

Vivi has finally confided in Richard, she thought. She was glad to know that he was still around and hadn't walked away from Vivi.

She looked around the room, politely greeting its occupants. She saw a couple whom she did not recognize but Vivi was not in the room.

Avoiding direct contact with Terry, she walked over to Richard who appeared to be agitated, "Richard where is Vivi? Is Brian going to be alright?"

Richard brows furrowed, "You knew about Brian?"

"Of course I know about Brian. Vivi told me about him couple of years ago."

Richard seemed more irritated by her response. Why did he seem mad that she knew about Brian? What was wrong with Vivi informing her about the little boy?

She was there to provide moral support to Vivi so she did not ask the questions puzzling her, like why wasn't he with Vivi anyway?

Instead she asked, "Where is she, Richard?"

He told her then walked away and began pacing the room again. Frowning at his strange behavior, she walked away to find Vivi. Perhaps he is finding it difficult to accept that she'd kept it a secret from him until now?

Abigail had stepped away to an adjourning room to take a call when Emmy entered the room.

She went over to Vivi and gave her a hug. She could see how worried Vivi was so she said to her, "Brian will be fine. I'm sure he has your strong will since he has your genes."

Vivi smiled. Neither of them was aware of the woman who had come out of the adjourning room and stood quietly watching them. She was glad that Emmy had come because it was the first smile she had seen on Vivi's face since she'd arrived at the hospital.

To cheer up Vivi even more Emmy said, "By the way I was surprised to see the Mcgallan clan camping out in the waiting room. Although I'd have to say the clan is not complete without the matriarch."

Vivi's smile widened then disappeared when she looked up to see Abigail standing in the doorway of the adjourning room. Abigail shook her head, signaling to Vivi that she should not disclose her presence.

Vivi hesitated to comply. What if Emmy made another comment about Abigail's family when she was earshot away?

But before she could say something Emmy went on to ask, "And why does Richard seem so irritated, anyway? Is he mad at the jerk that happens to be Brian's biological father or is he mad at you for not telling him until now?"

"Emmy, there's something you should know; something I just found out about an hour ago," she said.

"What is it?" Emmy asked.

"Emmy, Richard is Brian's biological dad."

Emmy was shocked but it explained Richard's previous question and behavior, "You mean he is ..."

A voice from behind her replied, "...the jerk who fathered Brian? Yes."

Emmy turned around and came face to face with Abigail Mcgallan. She was overcome with embarrassment that Richard's mom had heard her remark.

Abigail walked over to her and hugged her, "You must be Emmy, I've heard a lot about you. It's good to finally meet you."

Emmy was astonished by the hug especially since she had just referred to Abigail's son as a jerk.

"Hello, Mrs. Mcgallan. I'm afraid I haven't heard much about you so hopefully what you've heard about me has not included an embarrassing moment like this one?

Abigail chuckled, "Not really. I've heard only nice comments, here and there from Richard or Terry."

Emmy blushed at the mention of Terry's name and replied, "Contrary to what you heard, Richard is not a jerk but I'd have to say this is an interesting turn of events in this masquerade."

"It definitely is and I will leave you two to talk about that while I go to check on my clan," she chuckled.

She hugged Vivi and Emmy again, "I'm glad to have met you, Emmy. Thanks for coming to be with Vivi.

As Abigail was leaving the room, Terry walked in carrying a drink. She smiled and walked past him.

Terry walked over to Emmy, "Do you want something to drink?"

"Thanks but I don't drink coffee," she replied.

"I remembered. That is why I brought cappuccino."

"Thanks," she replied accepting the cup.

"You are welcome," he replied and left the room.

When she sipped the cappuccino, she couldn't help thinking that he had remembered not only that she didn't drink coffee but also just how she liked her cappuccino. She stared at his retreating form as he gently closed the door behind him.

"Men..." Vivi sighed, seeing the confusion all over Emmy's face, "Why are we always attracted to the ones that could cause us the most heartaches?"

"Because they make our hearts beat faster which makes us feel more alive."

Richard stood in the room looking down at his son. Brian had been moved from the recovery room but was still drifting in and out of sedation. He had not left the hospital since he learned he was the father of the child. Vivi had insisted that the Elliots go to get some rest and she had stayed but she had stepped out of the room briefly. His family had also gone but his mom had suggested that she and his dad would return so that Richard could get some rest also.

Brian stirred then his eyes fluttered open. He seemed more alert then he'd been the past hours.

"Where am I and why does my head hurt so much?"

Richard was at his bedside, reaching for his hand, "You fell off a bed and you are in the hospital. I'll call for your nurse right away."

"Are you my doctor? I remember you from the restaurant," Brian told him.

"I am not your doctor and yes I saw you at restaurant about a week ago."

"Then you are a stranger and I'm not supposed to talk to strangers."

"Actually he is not a stranger since you have a part of him in you."

It was Vivi who had returned from getting some fresh air. Richard turned and they stared at each other silently. Except for the occasional communication with the medical staff on Brian's status, they had barely spoken a word to each other.

"I do?"

She walked over to the bed and knelt by his side, "Yes, you do."

"What do you mean?" The child asked understandably unsure of the meaning of her statement.

Vivi knew he would have asked that. He was a smart kid so she'd expected that question from him but she was not the one who would tell him the actual reason. The parents he'd always known would have to make that call.

Her finger gently tapped his nose, "You see when you fell, you lost lot of blood and my friend, Richard, here was kind enough to give you some of his."

Vivi looked over at him and noted that he was not happy with her response. What did he expect? That she would tell the child "He is your biological father?" No, he would have to wait for Ben and Brenda to decide on how they wanted this revelation to go.

Brian looked up at him, "Thanks, Mr. Richard."

He wanted to tell Brian, call me dad but he couldn't so he answered, "I'll do that for you anytime you need it, kid."

"Aunt Vivi, did you know that I saw him at a restaurant?"

"I heard you did."

"And you seemed to have been having fun with that spaghetti judging from the way you were slurping it," Richard teased.

The child chuckled then winced, "Ouch."

"Why isn't the nurse here yet? I rang minutes ago," Richard complained.

"She is probably finishing up with another patient, Richard. I'm sure she will get here as soon as she can."

"Perhaps, he needs his own private nurse."

Vivi knew where he was going with that, "Don't even think about it," she warned.

The nurse walked in at that moment, "I see someone is up," she said cheerfully.

Chapter Fourteen

Richard glanced sideways at Vivi as they waited on the judge. He had followed through on his promise to file for custody. Despite her attempts to appear calm he could see that Vivi was tense.

"She had better be," he thought. After all he'd made an important phone call to a friend who owed him a favor. He trusted his friend would be in touch with the judge assigned to his custody case.

To weaken her composure even more, Richard pulled out an envelope and passed it on to Willie, his lawyer, "Could you pass this on to Ms. Whitman?

He watched as her eyes quickly read the letter Willie gave her. Then she looked over at him with disdain.

Vivi could hardly believe that Richard would go as far as terminating her employment at the company. But it was his company, wasn't? She told herself.

She was a lawyer and knew this was an attempt to ruffle her composure but she would not give him the satisfaction. Instead, she calmly slipped the enveloped into a folder. After taking a quick glance at him, she continued browsing through the pile of papers before her.

"All rise, Judge Sandra now presiding over the case of Mcgallan vs. Elliot.

The judge listened as both counselors presented their opening arguments. She'd gone over the case but was made even more aware of the nature of the case when she'd received a call from her boss.

She had her reputation to maintain so when both lawyers had presented their positions on the case she said, "Will both parties approach my desk, please?"

Sternly she warned them, "A child's well-being is at stake here. It is necessary that you put your own emotions and disagreements aside and consider what's best for him. I'll give you two weeks from today to work out an agreement or I'll be forced to settle this case here in the court."

She did not entertain questions as she instructed them to return to their seat.

"This court is in recess until two weeks from today," she told them bringing down the gavel.

As the echo of the gavel resounded in the court room, Vivi avoided Richards stare which was direct and piercing. He'd not had a ruling in his favor so she had to consider it a small victory for her in a way. She ushered her clients out of the courtroom and towards the stairs.

Richard met them at the top of the stairs. He greeted the Elliots courteously, inquiring on Brian's health then he turned toward Vivi.

"May I have a word with you, Elvira?"

She glared at him, "You can say what you want to say right here."

He shrugged, "Be ready at 7 o'clock this evening. I'll send a car for you and hopefully, we can work out some agreement.

"You're assuming I want to talk with you. Besides, shouldn't you be having that conversation—the work something out—with Brenda and Ben?"

"No, it was your decision to give up our child for adoption so it is you who will make this right. And believe me this is in keeping with the judge's request about reaching an agreement."

"It will have to be another day, Richard," she responded not wanting him to dictate to her. "I have a prior appointment."

"Then cancel it."

"No, I won't."

They engaged in a non-verbal duel, and then he asked the Elliots, "Is it possible for Brian to come over to my house for a short visit?"

"As your attorney, I will not advice that," Vivi told them.

She noticed the tightening of his jaw then he left them but not before he told Vivi, "See you at seven."

She stared after him, furious that he'd assumed she would do as he ordered. If he thought when he said "jump" she would simply ask "how high" then he had a surprise coming. She did not notice the exchange between the couple standing next to her.

***

Promptly at seven o'clock her doorbell chimed. She saw Martin, Richard's chauffeur, standing behind the door. Of course, she could not talk to Martin behind the door.

Vivi opened the door, "Martin, I'm so sorry he put you up to this. I told him I was not available today. Please let him know.

"Sure, Ms. Whitman."

She returned to the movie she had been watching on the television. She felt good that she had stood up to Richard and knew he would not like it. Her success was short lived when the doorbell rang again.

Surely, he did not send the older man to talk her into going?

When she arrived at the door, all she could see was a huge bouquet of roses with assorted colors.

"Ms. Whitman, I'm here to deliver these roses to you," a voice said.

She recognized the voice; it was William, Richard's chief of security. Richard knew the right surrogates to send, she thought. William had been so kind to her since she first met him on the day her fan belt had broken. She couldn't tell him to take the roses back to Richard.

Plastering a smile on her lips, she opened the door to let him in, "Thanks, William. You can set them on this table."

"Mr. Mcgallan sent them," William told her by way of explanation seemingly nervous.

"I know. Tell him I said thanks," she responded, trying to put up a civil front to William who was very loyal to Richard. She decided to trash it as soon as William left the apartment.

"You're welcome," was the response which startled her.

Now she understood why William had appeared uneasy. She had not seen nor heard Richard who had been following William. She'd left the door slightly ajar as she'd followed William to direct him to the table she wanted the flowers placed on.

"What are you doing here?" she asked Richard.

"We're meeting tonight to discuss our son's future. So you can come along willingly or I can carry you. The choice is all yours"

She was dressed in a pair of blue jeans that fitted her curves snugly. He'd seen her with jeans also when she was at his mansion—and like now, she looked fabulous in them. No, wonder she seemed to wear them often when she was not in the business suit for work.

"You have ten seconds if you want to change. He counted down the seconds silently all the time knowing she would not move from where she stood.

Vivi stood holding the door, waiting to shut it when Richard left. William had already walked out the door but hovered around as he usually did.

Richard's eyes scanned the living area and spotted her keys on the dining table. Walking over to it he picked it up and walked over to her.

He tossed the keys to William and lifted her effortlessly, "Lock up please, William," he instructed ignoring her objections and struggles as he carried her.

A while later, they were at his mansion she'd visited few weeks earlier. Why did he want them to dine at his mansion? Was it because she'd enjoyed her time here with him?

He had been quiet on the flight and seemed contemplative. But there was one occasion when she'd caught him staring at her with undisguised lust. He had not looked away when their eyes met but he'd reached out to trace the contours of her lips. He had leaned closer intending to kiss her. She'd felt her heart raced and she wanted him to kiss her but logic kicked in and she put some distance between them. She didn't want to give him the upper hand in negotiating Brian's future.

When they reached his home, Richard took her hand and led her to the dining room. He had purposely chosen to have dinner here because it would help her put into perspective the discussion they were about to have.

He pulled out a chair for Vivi, "Relax, Elvira, I will explain my proposition after dinner then I'll take you home."

His hand on her shoulder was reassuring and yielded the intended effect. The smell of the food made her realize she was hungry. She'd been in the process of thawing out her dinner when Martin had arrived at her apartment.

She sipped some wine before trying the entrees. She had some salad and garlic bread and skipped the saucy meatballs.

"Are you going to try the saucy meatballs?"

"No, salad's fine for me."

Richard took some meatballs and urged her, "You'll like it.

She refused his offer then asked, "What are we having for dinner?"

She decided Brian's future was more important than her disagreements with his dad. She would try to be amiable so that she could increase her chances of convincing Richard to do what's right for Brian.

"Lobsters—your favorite," he replied.

"How did you know that it's my favorite?"

Richard sipped some wine and held her gaze, "You told me the night Brian was conceived."

Vivi felt the blush rising, "Please, Richard, stop."

Temper flared as his gaze narrowed at her response. She couldn't be trying to avoid the very topic they had to discuss, he thought.

"Please stop what, Elvira? Please stop talking about our son? Or please stop reliving the night we spend together, nearly ten years ago?"

Her blush was clearly noticeable as he continued, "The truth is I can't help remembering every single detail of that night, even if I were to try to block it out which I won't."

Neither spoke as they stare at each other across the table. The tension that reverberated between them was only broken when the main course was served at that moment.

Elvira stood looking at the cozy fireplace and the surrounding rich décor in Richard's office. The last time she was in this room, they had been going over the legal papers for the new company he had purchased. But now she was very much aware of him after he'd made sure to remind her of their time together.

She wanted to have the discussion about Brian's future as soon as possible and be on her way. But Richard appeared to be in no hurry to begin as he refilled his now empty wine glass.

"More wine?" he asked her.

"Not for me, thank you."

He walked over to where she stood, "Tell me about him, Elvira. What was he like as a baby? How did he look?"

She lifted the heart-shaped locket on her chain and opened it to reveal the picture of Brian she'd carried everywhere she went.

Richard stared at the picture of his son for a while. Now he understood why her hand was always reaching for the necklace. He closed the locket and laid it against her cleavage, his hand unintentionally brushing her breast at he did so.

"You carried him against your breast but did he even have the opportunity of breastfeeding from them?"

Was that an undertone of implied criticism? She may have given Brian up but for the few months she'd had her son with her, she thought she was a good mother.

"Not that it's any of your business but I breastfed Brian until he went to his adopted parents. And if you don't mind, can you tell me your proposition?"

He walked over to the sofas on one end of the room.

"We will need to sit down," he said gesturing to the sofa.

She sat down on a sofa farthest from him. Sitting in another sofa, he studied her as he gathered his thoughts.

"I would like joint custody for Brian," he told her finally.

"I'm sure that can be arranged. I will talk about that with the Elliots."

He nodded. "That could mean they may have to relocate here. I am willing to cover the cost."

"They won't need your money."

His lips twitched in annoyance. Why was she rejecting his offer when it was made in good faith? He would not feel guilty for being wealthy. He'd earned his wealth so he ignored her comment.

"Brian will need twenty-four-hour security protection." He did not inform her that his team already had someone shadowing his son.

She made no comment. He was right. She had to face reality; Brian could become a target being the son of Richard Mcgallan.

"That's reasonable. I will get back to you once I have talked with Ben and Brenda."

Assuming the discussion was over she made to rise. His proposal was reasonable and she hoped the Elliot's would have no objections.

"One more thing," he added as she stood up.

She watched as he also rose to his feet. She had a premonition this final part of his proposal would not be favorable.

"I will not have sole custody of Brian so to compensate for that I realized I will need more kids."

So what does that have to do with me? She thought but before she could ask him that question she realized where he was going.

"No, you're not suggesting..." she told him.

"Yes, Elvira, you will bear two more children for me or I will take sole custody of my son."

He had some audacity, she thought so she responded, "Honestly Richard, I'm very sure that there are thousands of women out there who would gladly bear multiple babies for you."

"Yes, but only one woman will guarantee that Brian is loved and treated fairly as my oldest child. Once you have my kids, you're free to go."

She shook her head, "Please reconsider this proposal, Richard."

"No," he responded sharply. "Take it or leave it. You said you gave him up out of love for him. You will accept my proposal if you genuinely love him—unless I was right when I said you gave him up for your own selfish reasons?

"You're being very unfair and you know it," she told him. She grabbed her purse and walked towards the door, "I need to get home."

"I'll need your response on the anniversary of the date our son was conceived, Elvira."

She stopped and turned around to him, "That gives me only six days to think about this."

He smiled, "So you remember that day also. It was one very memorable night."

She did not respond but walked away. Tried as she might, she could not forget that incredible night with him.

Richard watched her go then he called and issued instructions that she be taken home.

Chapter Fifteen

Vivi presented Richard's proposal to the Elliots and they gladly accepted it as long as they could keep Brian. How could she deny them and her son from being together? She had had to make a sacrifice for him. So she had accepted Richard's proposition.

Brian thought his biological dad was cool and had no problem accepting the fact. He'd always called Ben, Papa, so he decided to call Richard, Daddy, to the delight of his birth father. The two were bonding, spending more time together and playing baseball which Brian was passionate about.

Richard convinced her to move in with him while they made the wedding arrangements—for safety reasons. He wasted no time in helping her plan a "small wedding" which contradicted her perception of small. He went with her to all the appointments besides the dress fitting. He wanted to have the dress makers come over to her but she had told him it would be more fun if she went to the shops to find her dress.

He'd insisted that she shopped at some specific dress shops which turned out to be the most expensive wedding dress shops. When she'd protested he had argued, "You can select whatever you want from among the variety of dresses. I don't care if it costs a penny or millions. Choose something you are comfortable with in style or cost."

So she had compromised. She would go to the shops he'd recommended but look for the least expensive dress that fitted her style.

Emmy had accompanied her and had insisted she found the perfect dress for her important day. The dress she finally settled on was a satin dress with an off-shoulder lace finish.

She had never thought her parents would have been in attendance but Richard had made a surprised visit to them without her knowledge.

Of course she had been furious when she had learned of it. He had told her he was going on a "business trip."

When he returned, he'd informed her, "Elvira, about the trip I just made... I went to meet your parents."

"You went to see my parents without informing me about your plans?" she had asked.

"I went to see your parents because I needed their permission to marry you. If I had a daughter and a guy married her without first asking me for her hand, I'd be enraged."

It sounded like an honorable gesture but it didn't change the fact that he went behind her back.

"Do you think they are going to think any highly of you knowing that I had a child for you and kept it a secret all these years?"

"I didn't tell them that but I think you should. It takes only one journalist to find out and the media will go crazy over the news."

"Whose fault is it going to be if the media gets hold of it, Richard? You could just have let things be as there were before you met Brian."

"I would never turn my back and pretend Brian didn't exist. You may have done that for nine years but I won't."

It was unfair but it came out before he could stop himself from lashing out. He saw her flinch then she got up and went towards the door without another word.

As she left his study he remarked, "Why is that not surprising —taking off in the middle of a discussion, I mean."

She turned to him, "This is not a discussion. This is what is referred to as an argument. Walking away is the logical thing to do in this case."

Two hours later, there was a knock on her door and he walked in.

"I know you love Brian, Elvira. I shouldn't have said that. Please accept my apology."

She was playing a crossword puzzle but she raised her head slightly to acknowledge him, "Apology accepted," she responded and turned her attention back to her game.

"They are your parents, Elvira. I will support you in whatever decision you make regarding Brian."

His pledge of moral support warmed her heart. She closed the book and stood up so that her eyes met his.

"You know I've kept it from them for such a long time, I'm worried even my mom will not be happy to hear she has a grandchild. My dad will definitely be infuriated."

"They love you, from what I gather, and that will never change. Try them. Whatever their response, you've got me on your side."

Richard took a step towards her. He needed to give her a hug, assure her of his support. Couple more steps and he was standing before her and his arms wrapped around her in a comforting embrace.

Vivi relished the deep enveloping warmth of comfort his embrace offered as she hugged him back. Suddenly she felt like she was ready to face the ghost of her past. She loved and missed her parents and the time was now to reconcile with them.

Still wrapped in his arms she announced, "I will go to find them tomorrow. They need to know about Brian."

"I'm coming with you."

He let her go and kissed her lightly on her forehead, "Get some rest. You have a long day ahead of you tomorrow."

She flew over to meet with her parents the next day. Richard was with her and she was greeted warmly by her parents. She had only communicated with them on the phone and made excuses when they had asked to visit her. They had respected her wishes.

"I've missed you so much, Vivi. Please don't stay away this long," her mother told her.

"I'll try to come home more often, mom. I promise," she replied.

"That's easy to say right now but once you're married and start having kids you might not be able to keep that promise," her father replied.

She looked over at Richard who had been quietly observing the family reunion. His expression was inscrutable.

She looked at her parents and hesitated. There seemed to be no easy way to tell them so she blurted out, "About that, dad, what if I already had a kid?"

"I see no wedding band so I will have to assume that you were not being serious," he told her looking from his daughter to Richard.

"You have a grandson, dad. He is nine years old and his name is Brian," she calmly responded.

Her parents were clearly taken aback but she saw her mother recover easily.

A smile began to form on her mother's face momentarily, only to be overshadowed by her dad's reaction. He seemed hurt or angry or both as he stood up.

"I'm going to my office and when I get back, I want you both gone," her father told them.

When he left the room she turned to her mom, "I'm sorry mom."

"No, I'm sorry I did not go to find you all these years. I think deep down my maternal instincts warned me that something was not right. But I was afraid of what I might uncover. Sorry, I wasn't there when you needed me most."

Lily went over and gave her daughter a warm embrace.

"I missed you, Mom."

"I love you, Vivi.

"Love you too, Mom.

"Always remember that no one is perfect; not even your father—the pastor," her mother said to her.

When her mother finally let her go, she realized Richard had left the room at some point to give them privacy.

"Tell me about my grandson," her mother said.

Vivi did and before long they were laughing and hugging just like old times.

Before she left, Vivi went over to her dad's office, knocked lightly, and went in after he gave his permission. She assumed he'd thought it was her mother.

"I thought I asked you to leave?" he asked when he saw her.

"I'm leaving, dad. I just wanted to apologize again for letting you down. I hope you can forgive me someday."

She'd left quietly hoping that he would come around soon. She wanted her dad at her wedding.

Brian was with them for the week of the wedding. The shared custody arrangement seemed to be working well.

Days before the wedding, her mother arrived. Lily had said she couldn't wait to see her grandchild.

Brian was upstairs in his bedroom when her mother arrived so she went to get him. Vivi met father and son engaged in a pillow fight. It seemed almost unbelievable that the stern powerful CEO of Mcgallan Corporation would be having such fun with his son. Parenting seemed to come naturally to Richard.

"Mom, watch out," Brian called out as one of the pillows came swinging towards her.

Brian had begun to call her mom which warmed her heart every time she heard him. After giving him up she'd never thought she would ever hear him say that precious three lettered word. Since he called Brenda, mama, he chose to call her, mom. They'd never talked about it but it had just happened one day when they were having dinner and her eyes had filled with tears. Richard had jumped in to distract Brian while she'd dabbed the tears away.

"Thanks for the heads up, Brian," she replied now as she tossed the pillow right back at his father.

She got caught up in the pillow fight until she accidentally tumbled on Richard as he fell onto a sofa.

He stirred into her eyes, the voice of their son "come on, let's play" faded into the distances. Neither of them moved nor spoke. Then she saw his face come closer to hers. Realizing their son was standing nearby she slid off him.

She looked at her son who was looking curiously at them, "Brian maybe you should change into something else to meet your grandma."

"Why? That looks good to me," Richard replied, standing up.

"That looks kind of creased, Brian."

"Relax, Elvira. He's meeting his grandma not Michelle Obama."

"I definitely agree with you, Richard," replied her mom who had come up to find them.

Moments later, Brian was enveloped in a loving hug. She saw tears roll down her mom's cheeks as she held her grandson close. Vivi reached for the tissue silently and her mother took it.

She was glad that she had listened to Richard's advice to come clean to her parents. She looked over at him and he must have sensed her gratitude because he walked over to her and his hand slid protectively around her. She leaned her head on his chest, glad that he was on her side. It dawned on her that she always wanted him there, right by her side always. She couldn't deny anymore that she was in love with him; she'd always loved him since she first met him."

On her wedding day, Elvira awoke early and looked through the window onto the driveway. Was her dad really not going to attend her wedding? She reached over to the bedside table for the picture she had of him and her mom.

Minutes later, her mom met her still holding on to the picture frame.

"Dad is not coming, is he?"

She knew this was just an arrangement between Richard and her but she'd hoped her parents would be there for her. She wasn't sure how Richard felt about her but for her since the day of her mother's arrival she knew she wanted to be with him for always.

"I'm sure he will show up. He might be stubborn but he loves you," her mother responded.

She had breakfast with her mother, Richard's mother, Meggie, and Emmy in her suite then she got dressed for her wedding. She was glad they were all there for her but it couldn't make up for her father's absence.

At the church, she stood with her mom waiting on the signal from the pianist when her dad walked through the doorway.

"Dad," her face lit up as she ran towards him.

"Hi, princess," he answered, as she was caught in his embrace.

"Thanks so much for coming," she told him feeling like the prodigal child.

"I'm so sorry, Vivi. What kind of pastor will I be if I don't practice what I preach? Besides, I would not miss that father and daughter dance for the world."

When she was much younger, they had practiced their father-daughter dance for her wedding day.

"Do you still remember it?"

"How could I forget it?"

Vivi hugged her parents close. It had been such a long time since they had had a group hug.

"I'd have to say you should thank that groom of yours for making me see reason. He can be quite persuasive."

Her dad explained that Richard had gone to see him at his church a day before the wedding. She looked over to where he stood in the church and her heart warmed to the man who had stolen her heart years ago. He was formidable but caring in his own way and she was proud that she was about to wed him.

Vivi walked towards him on the isle, knowing without a doubt that she wanted their marriage to last a lifetime. Did Richard feel that way also? She had no doubt he desired her but could it be more than that?

After their vows, when the pastor said, "I now pronounce you husband and wife, you may kiss the bride," she saw desire and something else flicker in Richard's eyes seconds before his lips ravished hers, teasing and coaxing.

It had been her dream wedding and there was nothing she would change about it. She closed her eyes as she leaned her head back, enjoying the therapeutic bath which was one of the amenities the hotel offered.

They were at the hotel where they'd first met. Richard had purchased it. The suite they had shared years ago was now the honeymoon suite at the hotel. It brought back so many memories; she felt butterflies flutter in her stomach in anticipation of their first night as a married couple.

Was that why she was taking a longer than necessary soak in the bathtub? Was it wedding jitters or was she afraid of her own response to him? Surely she couldn't stay in the bathroom all night?

She stood up and reached for a towel then she snuggled into her robe and walked into the room.

Richard was standing in the room when Vivi finally walked out of the bathroom. She looked beautiful and flushed in her silky red robe. Her hair hung loose on one shoulder.

She stood moistening her lips as he walked towards her. Was she even aware of how provocative she looked? Richard thought as the distance between them decreased.

Without a word he reached for the belt on her robe. With a little tug it came undone. His eyes feasted on her unfailing beauty.

She was more beautiful then he'd remembered. Could it be that giving birth to their son had enhanced her beauty? Her curves had been exquisite but now they were voluptuous and her breasts were fuller.

He touched one lightly and then the other, "You're incredibly beautiful, Vivi, he whispered.

Richard's hands slide beneath the robe and he pulled her to him. It felt so right to hold her so intimately after so many years. Her bare skin was warm to his touch yet he felt her shudder.

Vivi reveled in his warm embrace, leaning her head against his thudding heart. Her heart leapt in anticipation of what was to come. Would his heart meet hers halfway? Her hand came to rest on his heart, meeting his eyes.

"You don't know how much I have longed for this moment in the past years," he murmured as his lips sought hers.

His lips, when they claimed hers, were proprietary, hot, and inviting. Hers was accepting, warm, and as sweet as the honey he'd poured into her cup of coffee on the flight to their honeymoon suite.

She breathed in the spicy clean smell of his aftershave. Her arms came around his neck as he pulled her even closer. He was hers to have and to hold so she intended to enjoy their time together even if it were to only last up to the birth of their third child. She would accept whatever the future holds, just for this moment with him.

"Richard," she whispered his name as her robe fell to the floor.

"Elvira, my beautiful spitfire."

He carried her to the magnificent bed and laid her in the middle of the bed. She felt warmer with every touch of his exploring hands. The aroma from her soothing hot bath blended with the aroma emitting from the scented candles bathing the room in a warm glow.

She reminded him of a medieval queen upon whom her loyal servants waited. Tonight, he would succumb to her bidding, giving her all the pleasure he could possibly give her.

His hands explored her every familiar sensitive nerve and discovered new ones. She writhed with pleasure and her moans sounded like music being played by his warm delicate fingers.

She arched her back delightfully pulling him closer as her hands roamed over his back. Her nipples grazed his bare chest, hardening his loins and sending tremors throughout his body. Then his mouth found and feasted on them taking them one at a time while his skillful hands worked their magic on the other.

Richard sensed her eagerness as her hand reached for him, gently touching him. He gasped and clamped down on his lips. Then he reached for her hands, pinning them above her head while one leg came up to nudge her core. He would give her the completion she craved but he needed to sample every erogenous nerve until she begged for him to take her.

He wanted her so much he felt like he would explode if he didn't have her soon. But he had not forgotten the promise the made to her that she would have to beg him. He could not tell her but he would caress her until she could take it no more.

Vivi was nearing her peak and wondered why he was holding back, "Please, Richard," she begged.

"Please what, Vi?"

"Please, take me now. I can't take it anymore."

"Your wish is my command, my love. That's what I wanted to hear."

Then he pleasured her so that she was spinning on a whirlwind of

emotions until he caught up with her
and they sailed off unto their own
private oasis of fulfilment

Chapter Sixteen

Vivi stood few feet away watching women swarm over to Richard. They were attending a ball and she had excused herself to go to the lady's room where she had been awakened from her fantasy world. It was like a de'ja vu. She remembered the last time she had watched this scene play before her was at the charity ball.

Who really was the lady who had made her to face reality and why? It was just one day before they would be returning home from their honeymoon.

She had been happy and hopeful of their future until she heard the woman say, "There you are, Vivi—Richard's wife right?"

"Have we met before?" Vivi asked trying to be polite although she knew she hadn't met before.

"Not formally but it is sure nice to meet you finally. Who could have thought Richard would have gone through with his plan?"

Vivi felt chill go down her spin, sensing this would not be a favorable conversation, "What plan?"

"Richard always said he would do the right thing and marry the woman who had his first child to avoid inheritance conflict among his children."

Richard had explained that it was his reason for proposing marriage to her so why did it hurt coming from another woman? Was it because she'd hoped that he had proposed to her out of love and not what he had voiced to her? Well, she can put to rest that inkling of hope and close the chapter on her fantasy.

As she stood looking at the women flirting with Richard, the woman who had called herself Shannon murmured, "He's still quite a magnet attracting the most beautiful women in the hall. I'd say he still have eyes for them too."

Vivi watched Shannon disappear into the shadows. She walked toward Richard and saw him walk away from the women vying for his attention. He had eyes only for her as smiled in a way that made her legs feel like jelly.

When he said to her, "I'd say we call it a night," she nodded and allowed him to lead her out of the room and towards their waiting limo.

It was obvious she was the envy of all the women in the room. She saw the looks that came her way and the looks directed towards their entwined hands as they exited the room. When they had walked into the ballroom earlier, she'd been confident but she left feeling like Cinderella leaving the ball after the clock struck twelve.

When they returned home after the honeymoon, Richard worked long hours to get caught up with work that needed his immediate attention. He felt guilty that he was not spending enough time with his new bride so to make it up to Vivi he returned home early one afternoon, intending to surprise her.

Vivi had decided to start her private practice since she was not working at Mcgallan Corporation. She had been spending long hours in her home office so he headed there to find her but she was not there. He learned from a house staff that she was not home.

He called her chief bodyguard who informed him that she was having lunch with a friend at one of her favorite restaurants. He wasn't sure why he'd asked if it was a male or female friend but he didn't like hearing that it was a guy. He stormed out of the house and was on his way to the restaurant.

The ride to the restaurant felt like the longest ride Richard had ever taken. Was she having an affair? If so how long had it been going on? Is that why she seemed to be withdrawn since their return home? Why hadn't someone given him a heads up?

He knew her bodyguards owed their loyalty to her and they were not his spies but didn't they owe him some loyalty too. After all, wasn't he paying their salaries? He didn't want to be a controlling husband but maybe he should tell them to inform him whenever she left the house.

Richard did not wait for his security to open the door to the limo. He was out as soon as the vehicle came to a stop.

"Thanks for meeting with me, Randy," Vivi said to her colleague.

They had been friends in law school and sometimes sought each other advice on cases. He was one of the few college friends she'd invited to her wedding. She was glad that he worked close by.

"Of course, I was surprised to hear from you. I had assumed you may have forgotten about the friends you met along the way."

"What's that supposed to mean?"

"Just that you are the wife of a very wealthy man and I don't suppose he would want you meeting with me."

"This is a business meeting and my husband trusts me."

"That is what you said so does that mean that you are not working at your husband's company?"

Vivi did not want to go into that discussion with him so she answered, "I'm looking into starting my own practice so I thought you might be able to give me advice since you just went through that process."

"Or better yet we could become partners since I am still looking for qualified partners."

It was a thought she had not considered. Randy was a good lawyer and she would not mind a partnership with him. But she wondered if Richard would have reservations.

Before she could respond Randy continue, "I understand you would have to talk it over with your husband but let me know your decision. You would make a great law partner."

"I'm sure Richard will have no problem with it but I will have to think about your offer and determine if it will be the right career path for me."

"I'm not so sure your husband will be open to that idea."

"How would you know that?"

"Let's just say our lunch is over."

He was looking in the direction of the entry way. Vivi turned slightly and saw Richard striding towards them purposefully.

"Dawson."

"Mcgallan."

Both men acknowledged each other as Vivi sat, knowing Richard had come to get her.

"We're leaving now, Elvira," Richard told her leaning over to kiss her fully on the lips.

Was he trying to make a statement to Randy? What would happen if she told him she was in a meeting and she would be leaving as soon as she was done? She wouldn't ask him to leave a business meeting if the tables were turned, would she? She knew she would be right to stand up to him but not here in the public when there could be a reporter lurking somewhere.

She didn't want that publicity so she stood up. Randy stood up also and watched as Richard pulled the chair for his wife to leave.

"I'll call you with my decision on the partnership, Randy."

"No, you won't. And don't even attempt to contact my wife, Dawson. You don't want me coming after you."

Randy did not feel threatened by Richard and simply responded, "Vivi can make her own decisions."

"Don't even try crossing me Dawson, you'd be surprised what I'm capable of doing to your career," Richard replied not waiting for Randy's response as he led Vivi away.

Vivi was furious with Richard and sat quietly the entire trip home. Richard made no comment either as he tried to analyze why he was so enraged with jealousy when he walked into the restaurant and saw his wife having lunch with another man.

He looked across at her as she tried to avoid any physical or visual contact with him. She was mad at him and she probably had every right to be. It scared him as he realized there was only one reason why he had been so jealous—he was afraid of losing her. He was crazy in love with her. He had been for many years now, he admitted.

Vivi could not wait to get out of the limo when it came to a stop. Ignoring his attempt to help her out of the limousine she hurried into the house greeting the butler who had held open the door for her.

Richard hurried after her, "Enough of the silence, Elvira. I suggest we go to my office and talk.

"Not now, I need some time to myself," she responded as she climbed the stairs to their master suite.

He had been a little domineering so he decided to give her some time. He went to his study and delved into work but after an hour of getting no work done he went in search of her.

She was in the sitting area working on a crossword puzzle. He smiled as she made no attempt to acknowledge his presence.

"You can have your job back at the company."

"And have you fire me again at will? No, thank you."

She did not raise her head from the puzzle as she responded.

"I don't want you partnering with him."

"Then I'll start my own practice."

"I'm sure you can. I'll support you one hundred percent on that."

He walked over to her and a finger lightly traced the outline of her neck. Unable to resist his touch, she raised her head. He lowered his head and captured her lips.

"Maybe... I should... start working... on my practice."

He pulled her out of the chair and carried her to their bedroom, "I promise to let you to do that but first..."

Brian ran ahead of Richard into the house. Excited and full of energy, he went to Vivi's office but saw that she was not in her office like she usually was. He was going fishing with his father and uncles.

"Dad," he called out to Richard, "where's mom?"

"Check in her office."

The boy appeared at the top of the stairs, "She is not there," he told his father.

Richard was concerned so he ended his conversation with his butler and hurried up the stairs. The butler had said she had not gone out.

"Come on let's go and find her, son. She might be in our suite."

Brian ran ahead shouting, "Mom."

Vivi stirred then her eyes blinked open as she heard Brian's call, "In the room Brian," she called out.

Brian went into the room followed by Richard. Elvira sat up as Brian climbed onto the bed.

She hugged him, "Hey buddy."

"I'm going fishing today with dad and my uncles."

"So I heard. I'm looking forward to cooking your fish when you get back."

He turned to his father, "You will show me what I need to do to catch a fish right, dad."

"I sure will, son," Richard responded, taking his eyes off Vivi to smile at his son.

He was concerned that Vivi was asleep at that time of the day. Of late, she had been sleeping more than she had done before. He would come home some evenings and find her asleep in the chair in her office. He would carefully carry her to bed and she would only slightly stir then fall back to sleep. He thought she was working hard spending long hours trying to get her practice up and running.

He had tried to send clients her way but she had objected saying, "Richard, I know you want to help but I can't take the clients you are sending my way."

"What makes you think that I'm sending clients your way?" He had thought she might reject his help so he had tried to be discrete.

"Aren't you?"

He leaned back in his chair and replied, "Okay, I may have suggested that you have started your practice."

"I want to be successful because I'm good at my job, not because I am your wife."

He nodded, "I promise I won't intervene anymore."

"Thanks," she told him and walked way.

Then she stopped and turned around to him, "You are aware the clients you sent my way might all be retiring soon and their next of kin would be taking over right?"

"What is that supposed to mean?"

"I would inevitably have met their successors."

A grin formed across his face. He had carefully referred only older clients but she was smart enough to know why.

"You can't blame me for trying to protect my wife from the sharks out there," he had responded reminding her of her insinuations on the day they met at the ball.

She had giggled and left the study. His own laughter echoed in the study as he got back to work. Each day his love for her grew even when she was challenging him.

Now as he looked at her deep in conversation with their son, he wondered if he could convince her to cut down the hours she spent at work. She didn't need to work but he valued her sense of independence. He hoped she would not over work herself.

Hoping to talk with her before they left, he said to Brian, "Brian do you want to play a quick game on the Wii before we leave?"

"Yes, please."

"Why don't you go and get it set up then."

"Which game should we play, dad?"

"You choose, son."

As soon as Brian left Richard turned to her, "Are you okay? We can reschedule the trip if you don't feel well."

"I'm fine, really. Brian is looking forward to this trip. I have only been sleeping a lot lately."

"And eating a lot more," Richard replied.

He'd noticed that and now he wondered aloud, "Are you pregnant?"

Surprised that he had mentioned what she had not been thinking she responded, "No, I don't have any morning sickness or anything of that sort."

It didn't seem like the response he had hoped for. She was right. Wasn't morning sickness the biggest indicator of pregnancy?

"Alright, as long as you're sure..."

"I'm sure."

He gave her a one over, seemingly not convinced but accepting her response.

"I should go to keep my promise of that game with Brian."

As soon as Richard left the room, Vivi began checking her calendar and counting down the days. Four days past her scheduled date but wasn't it sometimes plus or minus couple of days or more? She leapt out of bed knowing she had to make sure with a pregnancy test.

Chapter Seventeen

Positive! Positive!

The test results read. She had waited until Richard and Brian left then she'd gone to the store to purchase the tests. She bought two tests—to be sure.

She touched her stomach, gently. Their baby was growing in her belly.

I will have to set up an appointment for the hospital, she thought.

She called her doctor then went to look up nutrition facts for an expecting mom. It had helped her to eat right when she was carrying Brian but she could not remember it anymore.

Richard had been right. She was pregnant. How should she inform him of the good news? Maybe she could leave the test tubes on the sink in the bathroom?

When she went into the kitchen later to help with dinner like she always did, Lorraine, the cook, had a snack waiting for her.

Lorraine ushered her to the kitchen island and urged, "Have a snack while I chop the veggies. You need to eat well so that the baby is healthy."

"Thanks, Lorraine."

She looked up at Lorraine, "Wait you know?"

"I've suspected that you were expecting a child for about a week now."

"How, I have not been having morning sickness."

"I'm a mother of two and there are other signs other than morning sickness.

Vivi was hungry so she dug into the sandwich. She still had not figured out a way to tell Richard and they would be returning soon.

"How did you tell your husband?"

"Oh, I had my ways. Just follow your instincts."

Brian brought home a large Tilapia which Vivi seasoned and fried then soaked in her own special sauce.

"I've never had a fish this delicious," Brian said as they were eating.

"That's probably because you caught the fish yourself."

"That plus this sauce is good with it."

"I couldn't agree more, Brian," Richard replied.

"Dad, we should probably go fishing more often," Brian said to Richard.

"We definitely will, son."

Viv smiled, glad that the bond they shared with Brian grew each day, "And I'll look forward to cooking it whenever you get back."

The rest of the meal went by as if they had always been together as a family since his birth. They later went into the living room and played some board games. It wasn't long before Brian was falling asleep in his chair.

Elvira said, "Why don't you go on up and get ready for bed, Brian. I'll be there shortly to tuck you in."

When Brian left to get ready for bed, Richard poured himself a drink then offered her a glass of wine also. He had not noticed that she had not had the wine he'd poured at the dinner table. Thanks to Brian's banter.

When he brought the drink over to her she shook her head, "I can't have it for the next nine months."

His eyes lit up, "Are you..."

"Yes, you were right. I'm pregnant— at least according to the two over the counter tests. I have..."

She did not complete the last sentence as his arms encircled her and his lips claimed hers.

It was a long time later before she continued, "I've made appointment to see my doctor."

"Can we tell Brian that he's going to be a big brother?"

"I think we should wait until after the hospital appointment."

His lips claimed hers again, "In that case, we should both go and tuck him in then we can continue this conversation in the comfort of our room. He held her hand as they walked up the stairs and to Brian's room.

Vivi smiled as she walked towards Richard. They were on their way to her first prenatal doctor appointment. The hospital test had shown that she was indeed pregnant.

She was wearing a pair of tights and a sleeveless flowery top. She had begun to wear maternity clothing because she felt like she could already see the baby bum.

Richard felt she always made the most casual outfit look classy. "You look beautiful," he told her sliding his arm around her.

"Thank you."

The joy they shared knowing they were expecting a baby was obvious in the looks and smiles they exchange as well as their lingering touches at every chance they got. Richard was tender and kind showing her by his every action that he cared. Vivi felt cherished and loved even though he made no declaration of love.

Richard could see that his intent to convince Vivi of his love was well on track. Did she feel the same way about him or was she just being nice? He could sense that she cared about him but her intent on being independent made him concern that she had no intention of a "forever after" with him. He decided he would never know unless he took his chance and professed his love for her. It would have to be once they return home from her appointment today.

***

Twins! The doctor announced. He had heard two heart beats and excitedly gave them the news.

"Definitely two heart beats. Congratulations, you are having twins."

"Are you sure?" Richard had asked.

"Definitely but if you'd prefer a second opinion I'll call in a colleague if it is okay with you."

Richard nodded so another doctor had come in and confirmed it was two heartbeats.

Vivi looked over at Richard who appeared tense, "We can handle twins, can't we?"

His smile, "We sure can."

She felt some change come about him. Of course he wasn't worry about the expenses that came with having multiple babies. He had more than enough to care for quintuplets. So what was it? Perhaps he would tell her in the car on their way home? But he didn't.

Richard was quiet on the way home. Nine months was the only time he would have with Vivi if she didn't love him enough to stay with him. He had been willing to take his chance before this appointment but now he wasn't quite sure. She seemed happy to be carrying twins. Was she ready to be rid of him? If so, he couldn't bear her rejection. Perhaps, he would be wise to stick to their original plan?

Vivi noticed that the change that had come about Richard remained even though he tried to act as if nothing had changed. She wished he would let her know his concerns.

At dinner, their conversation was polite and strained for a couple who had been married for nearly three months. She couldn't bear the distance that had come between them so she excused herself after dinner and went to bed.

Richard watched her go. He wanted to go after her and beg her to forget about the agreement and stay with him but he didn't.

Vivi awoke in the middle of the night and noticed Richard had not come to bed. Okay, she thought, I need to know why the sudden change so she went in search of him.

She found him asleep in the guest room. When she switched on the light in the room, Richard woke up and seemed concerned. He got out of the bed and went over to her.

"Are you alright?" he asked her.

"It depends," she answered.

He frowned in concern, "What's going on?"

"Actually, that is a question I would like you to answer. A change has come about you since we learned we were having twins. What's *your* problem?"

He rubbed his head but did not respond so she continued, "I'm going to bed and you might want to come to bed—in the master bedroom where we have been sleeping these past months. Just in case you forgot."

"Can't you see that is my problem?"

"What's that supposed to mean."

"If I come to bed with you, I can't keep my hands off you and I won't be able to let you go again."

Was he trying to tell her what she had been hoping to hear? She couldn't afford to make assumptions. In her business, facts not assumptions made a good case.

The lawyer in her took over. It was the case of her heart and she couldn't afford to lose.

"Why, Richard? Why won't you be able to let me go?"

"Because I love you, Vivi."

He reached for both of her hands, "I'm crazy about you. I really hope you feel the same about me. Even half as much will be enough for me."

She had just been listening and staring at him, unable to speak. Then she stood on tippy toe and kissed him.

"I never thought I would ever hear you say that. I have loved you for many years since we first met."

He pulled her close, "I searched everywhere for you when you left. That is why I bought the hotel. I hoped that you would go there and that we would be able to meet there again."

"I didn't know you were searching for me. I'm sorry I didn't use the charm to find you."

"Speaking about charm," he pulled out a box from his pocket and took out a chain, "now that our son has the original charm, I made this one for you."

He opened the box and fastened the chain to her neck. It was a gold chain with a solid diamond star.

"I love you so very much," he said hoarsely.

Her hand caressed his face gently, "I love more."

Richard scooped her in his arms, "That is an argument you'll have to defend for the rest of our lives, counselor."

"I'll be obliged to," she responded as she her hands encircled his neck.

Key to Her Heart
By
Elin Magdalene

Dedicated to all who dream big the
American way
May your dreams come true

Chapter One

Terrance Mcgallan glanced quickly at his wristwatch and stood up. There were still empty chairs but he assumed everyone who needed to be present was already in the room. They had trickled in gradually but were finally all there—hopefully. He walked over to the door and closed it decisively.

"Okay, I believe we can start the meeting now."

Willie, one of the employees looked around the table, "Umm, I think Emeline is on her way. Perhaps we should wait on her."

"It is a minute past the time we should have begun. She can join us later. We will begin with the chief accountant's presentation," he dismissed the suggestion.

The room was quiet as the employees stared at each other. He waited to hear from the chief accountant.

"Actually, Emeline *is* the chief accountant," one of the ladies responded.

Before he could respond, he heard the clickety, click sound of a lady's stilettos drawing near the closed door.

He walked towards the door, hoping to stare down this chief accountant who presumably had no respect for time. He pulled open the door, totally unprepared for the beauty that greeted him with an unusual gingered color hair.

"Hi, sorry I'm late," she apologized cheerfully as if it were no big deal that she was late for the meeting.

She looked breathtakingly gorgeous. Am I awake? Terry wondered or did I just fall into a trance? He recovered smoothly but had she noticed his reaction?

He'd seen many beautiful women but no one as stunning as this one so it was almost refreshing to just gaze upon her. He gawked into her sensual dreamy eyes, shaped like an almond. Those were the highlight of her face and her lips were as full as the carpel of a juicy, ripe orange. Were they as tasty as the fruit would be in full bloom? He realized he was staring so he stepped aside to let her into the room.

She exuded warmth and energy. Suddenly, it seemed like a ray of sunshine had streamed through the open blinds making the room seem brighter and warmer. He heard the room come alive as he turned around.

She chatted away greeting each person and apologizing to the group. She laughed as they chided her about her tardiness.

"I apologize again. I promise to work on it."

"You will definitely need to if you want to work for Mcgallan Corporation."

That was the response from the man who had opened the door for her. The room became quiet again.

Emeline turned her attention to the man speaking to her. Standing at about 6"9' and a shoulder width nearly the length of her arm, he filled the room. No doubt, his suit was tailored especially for him. He was powerfully built with a dashing physique so that she found herself wondering if she should have waited a month longer before accepting Ryan's proposal.

She caught herself on the thought. Was she already having second thoughts about her engagement just because of a stranger? Granted there was no harm in appreciating a hunk but having second thoughts about one's fiancé? That was not what a woman in love would do. She shook off the thought and opened her mouth to respond to him.

"Actually, I work for my grandfather and he doesn't mind if I am a minute or two late for a meeting."

"It's more than a minute or two late and I hate to be the one to tell you but your grandfather just signed over his company to Mcgallan Corporations."

She didn't believe him so she took out her phone dialed her grandfather. He had gone on vacation to the Caribbean but he always picked up her calls wherever he was. This time, the call went to his voicemail so she called again but got the voicemail a second time. She panicked, wondering if he was okay.

Terry watched her attempt to call her grandfather. He went over to his seat, opened a folder and took it over to her. Emeline looked over the legal documents and noted that it had being signed that day.

She still needed to know that her grandfather was okay so she excused herself, "I need to make a call."

"You've already wasted enough time making calls. I need to see the financial report and I'm sure my secretary communicated with you the urgency of this request."

"I need to know that my grandfather is alright. This has nothing to do with doubting you or these documents. He always takes my call so this is a first for me. I will be back as soon as I know he is good. Please excuse me for a minute."

Emmy did not care that under the circumstances she could get fired for insubordination. She was concerned about her grandfather not her job. After all he was the only family she had and it was unlike him to ignore her call. In fact he would stop in the middle of negotiations to take her call.

Her mood change could be compared to dark clouds hovering over the sun on a sunny day. Terry couldn't explain what may have influenced his next action except to tell himself that he needed to get on with the meeting. He picked up his phone and dialed

242

Howard's number. The older man answered the call on the first ring.

"Howard, someone would like to talk to you."

Terry handed her the phone and was pleased with the relieve that overcame her. He couldn't suppress the joy that tugged at his heart when he realized he'd done something she appreciated.

"Grandpa, are up okay?" I was worried sick and would have taken the next flight if you had not responded."

She listened to him then responded, "We have to talk but I will call later. Make sure to answer your phone or I'll be there on the next flight and will not return without you."

She hung up minutes later and murmured thanks as she gave Terry his phone. Then the perkiness was back in her voice and all about her.

He looked at his watch and noted that he had spent nearly ten minutes trying to mollify Emeline Weisener. He knew he would go out of his way to see her light up the room any day and it bothered him. Why should he care that she was spoiled rotten?

Emeline wasted no time but went up to present the report requested. It was the best presentation he'd seen a chief accountant make. She responded knowledgeably to the questions asked providing detailed information.

Terry was glad that the meeting had gone well besides the setback with Emeline at the beginning. He still had one matter to take care of. He wanted her to know he expected nothing less than hard work and efficacy from his employees.

He would be her immediate supervisor so he wanted to establish some guidelines without necessarily spelling it out. Besides her report was so clean that he had to check beyond the three years point to identify any flaws which may have been covered.

As was her entrance, she was the last employee to exit the room which was fine by him this time around. Before she could leave the room he stopped her, Ms. Weisener, may I have a hard copy of the monthly reports from the last five years, please?

"You can't possibly mean the monthly report from the last *five* years?"

"Yes, I mean exactly that. Will that be a problem for you?" He challenged her, holding her gaze.

She shrugged, "No, I was just asking to make sure I understood you right."

There was the sound of the keyboard clicking then the printer in the conference room began to spit out papers.

"Well, there go the reports you requested. Do you want me to stable them together as well?"

"No, thanks."

Emmy went to the printer and stood waiting for the papers so that she could take them to Terry. She thought watching the papers fall out of the printer was better than sitting at the table with him.

Terry felt he could wait for the papers and she could get on with her work so he walked over to the printer.

"I can get them..."

She had not heard him come up behind her until he spoke. Startled she jumped, falling into his arms as she turned around.

Emmy stared into the most amazing large brown eyes she'd ever seen. He held her gently but firmly and his eyes roamed over her. Strangely, she felt as if she belonged in his arms. It was a thought that frightened her yet she made no attempt to extricate herself. She'd never felt this way in Ryan's arm. Was it wrong to feel this way in another man's arms?

Why did he smell so good as if he'd just showered minute ago? The aroma of lavender with sandalwood and another spice filled her nose. It emphasized his masculinity and heightened sensual awareness. She could not resist the thought of these powerful arms tenderly exploring her body.

Terry held on to Emeline, feeling proprietary for the first time in his life. It was mind boggling for him since he did not know her. She was soft, excitingly warm, and admirably glamorous. Why was she having such effect on him?

He never lacked the attention of beautiful women but it was more than her beauty that attracted him. Her mouth was inches away from his. He was tempted to have a taste of her lips. Didn't his brother require of him a no-employee policy for his affairs? Why did he think this would be the first time he went against his brother's wishes on that policy? He thought as he let her go.

"Sorry, but I'm engaged," he heard her say raising her left hand to show him when she was out of his arms.

Did she just remember her engagement now when she'd seemed willing to remain in his arms earlier? How had he not noticed the ring on her left finger? Was it because he had been so busy admiring her captivating beauty or was it because he did not want to see it?

"How convenient that you just remembered that commitment."

She stepped away from him and went to get her computer and notepad then she walked to the door. She stood for a while then walked back to where he stood arranging the papers he'd taken out of the printer.

"Here, you might need this," she told him, holding out a key.

Terry held out his hand and she placed the key in his hand. The key had a heart-shaped bow. He stared at it.

"What do I need this for?"

"It is the key to a room in the basement of this building where I keep the hard copies of invoices since I began working here. You might need that while you conduct an audit on the financial reports."

She walked away leaving him to stare after her retreating radiance. He gave her a one-over noting the killer stilettos she was wearing. He felt the heels were unreasonably high for comfort but she appeared comfortable walking in them. Her legs did justice to the stilettos but even more enthralling was her tantalizing feminine curves.